REDHEAD

John Creasey

Master crime fiction writer John Creasey's 562 titles have sold more than 80 million copies in over 25 languages. After enduring 743 rejection slips, the young Creasey's career was kickstarted by winning a newspaper writing competition. He went on to collect multiple honours from The Mystery Writers of America including the Edgar Award for best novel in 1962 and the coveted title of Grand Master in 1969. Creasey's prolific output included 11 different series including Roger West, the Toff, the Baron, Patrick Dawlish, Gideon, Dr Palfrey, and Department Z, published both under his own name and 10 other pseudonyms.

Creasey was born in Surrey in 1908 and, when not travelling extensively, lived between Bournemouth and Salisbury for most of his life. He died in England in 1973.

THE DEPARTMENT Z SERIES

REDHEAD

JOHN CREASEY

ipso books

This edition published in 2016 by Ipso Books

First published in Great Britain by Hurst in 1933

Ipso Books is a division of Peters Fraser + Dunlop Ltd

Drury House, 34-43 Russell Street, London WC2B 5HAk

CONTENTS

x

1

MARTIN STORM IS ANNOYED

The two men lolling against the white rails of the *Hoveric* and gazing dreamily across a widening expanse of water to a grey smudge which an hour before had been easily recognisable as Cherbourg, might well have been mistaken for brothers. Both possessed dark hair, blue eyes flecked with grey, pleasing, irregular features and a physical springiness that even in repose was notable.

There was one physical difference between them, however. Martin Annersley Storm, popularly known as Windy, was two inches taller and proportionately larger than Robert Montgomery Grimm, as popularly called Grimy. In point of fact they were cousins, and if a stranger had overheard parts of their conversation during their lighter moments he might have been forgiven for imagining that their greatest aim in life was to see the last of each other in the least possible time. Nothing could have been farther from the truth.

As they basked in the warm sun they were acutely aware of two things.

Primarily, that the first class sports deck on which they lolled was a vast improvement on the third class steerage which had sheltered them during the voyage from New York to Cherbourg.

The second, that the man with the flaming red hair who was absorbing most of their attention, was extremely popular.

As they looked on, Ginger was performing prodigious feats of strength with a twenty-eight pound iron ball and a vaulting horse brought from the gymnasium for his especial benefit. The point which vaguely annoyed both Storm and Grimm was the revolting enjoyment which he derived from basking in the adulation of an admiring crowd.

After twenty minutes of watching this untiring behaviour, Storm took his pipe from his mouth and remarked mildly;

'Uppish cove, the Ginger bloke.'

'I'd like to poke him one,' Grimm muttered, and from this comparatively long speech Storm knew that the spark of dislike which Ginger had ignited in his own breast had a fellow in Roger Grimm's.

The mutual love of Martin Storm and Roger Grimm for a beano had come within an ace of proving fatal during their stay in New York. A casual, and rather contemptuous reference to 'gangsters' had been taken amiss.

Seven days before embarking on the *Hoveric* they were halfway along a comparatively quiet road from Manhattan to Long Island when something went wrong with their engine.

Then a bullet smashed through the windscreen, cracking against the coachwork, setting up little spurts of dust in the dry road and whirling the startled Storm's hat high into the air. After the first second of stupefaction Storm, crouching low, bellowed a warning to Grimm and drove recklessly into some trees at the side of the road. Like a reluctant turtle the Packard heeled on one side before crashing into the trees. Beneath it, sandwiched tighter than any sardines but much more lively, Storm and Grimm crouched, helpless but fluent.

Though Grimm had recently won a much prized trophy downtown from a world famous heavyweight, all the boxing skill in the world would have been useless against the fusillade from the machine-gun which was being fired from a stationary car twenty yards ahead, and after an interminable barrage they heard the cessation of the deadly tap-tap-tap with heartfelt relief. But they were chalking something up against the gentry; if they had known where it was going to lead them they would have chalked still more furiously.

There followed, after rescue by a passing motorist and a small army of police which had appeared with surprising celerity, a somewhat hectic interview between Storm, as the spokesman of the cousins, and Superintendent O'Halloran of the New York Police. O'Halloran, a big, bluff man with close Irish Republican connections and a carefully nurtured dislike of all Englishmen who didn't drop their aitches, was talkative but unhelpful.

'Sure,' he admitted, 'the bhoys that tried to get ye got away wid it. What wud ye expect? But we've an idea who they were, Mr Storm, don't ye worry.'

'I'm not worrying,' said Storm grimly. 'But it seems to me that you should be. Who was it? And what was the complaint?'

O'Halloran played irritatingly with a petrol lighter.

'As for who it was, Mr Storm, it'd be bad cess to the man as gave them a name without being sure! As for why they picked ye out – '

With an unpleasant grin splitting his thick features he shifted an untidy heap of papers and pulled out a column from *The Courier* which had been cut from a recent issue. After the historic fight which had robbed America of the prized boxing trophy Grimm was a nine days' wonder, and the newspapers' eulogies included Martin Storm. Both had suffered one interview with the Press. One bright spark – *The Courier's* man – had demanded their views on the gangster problem.

And on the following morning a thousand word story was splashed on the front page, which story Superintendent O'Halloran was now fingering.

It ran:

BOXING ENGLISHMEN'S CHALLENGE TO GANGS
'LET 'EM ALL COME' SAYS MARTIN STORM.
ROGER GRIMM, NEW CHAMP, JUST GRINS
The Courier in an exclusive interview with the famous English amateur boxing giants who have just staggered America, Martin Storm and Roger Grimm, learned that neither of these wonderful fighters gives much heed to the gangster menace. 'In England' says Mr Storm, 'we put them where they belong – in jail, with the rest of the small rogues and pick-pockets who prey on humanity. If they show fight – well, what've we got fists for?'

He had said nothing of the kind. But a protest would have brought the whole of the popular Press squealing about their ears, and they had had far too much publicity already; the notice was allowed to pass without complaint.

Storm kept cool with difficulty as he eyed O'Halloran.

'No one took any notice of that tripe, did they?'

'Well, Mr Storm – ' O'Halloran lit a cigar, half-closing his eyes as he leaned back in his chair and rolling the 'Mr Storm' with a calculated insult perfected only by the less pleasant type of Irishman. 'What else wud ye expect? Ye hit them on the raw and they hit ye back.' He opened his eyes suddenly, leaning forward and pushing the cigar an inch from Storm's nose. 'Take it from me, and get away while ye can. Ye're lucky to be alive, an' it's me that says so! Meanwhile ye can rest in peace, for I'm looking after ye.'

Storm rose furiously to his feet.

'Steady,' cautioned Grimm, knowing Storm's happy knack of kicking up a first-rate shindy. 'Leave it, old boy.'

That Grimm's counsel prevailed had no beneficial effect on Storm's frame of mind as he strode along Broadway. It was an unfortunate initial experience of the American police, and his views on that excellent but sorely tried body of men would probably have been even fiercer had he known that several tough-looking hobos lurching behind and in front of him were plainclothes members of the force keeping a sharp eye open for any possible 'accident'.

Less than an hour afterwards, sitting opposite Grimm at the Forty Club, a paragraph in *The Courier* caught his eye. With a snort he handed the paper to his cousin. Grimm read on with tightening lips.

ANOTHER GANG WAR?

A private car whose owner is unknown was fired on and overturned on the Baldwin, Long Island road late this morning. The occupants escaped but avoided the police, who are ignorant of their identity. It seems that this is a fresh outbreak of warfare between rival gangs....

'Ump,' he commented. 'Funny.'

Storm scowled.

'Funny's one way of putting it,' he admitted. 'It at least makes it clear that O'Halloran doesn't want the Press to know who the occupants of the car were. Ask yourself, Roger, why shouldn't the whole world know? No reason at all, unless it's to save us from publicity, which is bunk! No – that dear little Superintendent wants to push us out of the country with little fuss and less Press notice. He doesn't want any shindy kicked up about this afternoon's little wallop. That's plain enough, isn't it?'

'Vaguely,' Grimm admitted. 'But what's the idea?'

'That,' said Storm with some annoyance, 'is the kind of dam' fool question you would ask. Because I can't answer it. But I can tell you one thing. O'Halloran is in for the surprise of his life if he thinks we'll take the hint.' He jerked Grimm's elbow. 'Start moving, my lad!'

'Where to?' demanded Grimm with excusable curiosity. 'Besides, I want another drink.'

'You can want on,' said Storm. 'We're going to have a chat with the bonny boys of *The Courier.*'

Twenty minutes later he was agreeably surprised at the news editor's almost effusive greeting. They were put in charge of a harassed man in shirt-sleeves, who cocked a knowing eye when he heard their names and conducted them through a maze of tables in a vast office. Two dozen men and half-a-dozen stenographers were talking at the same time, bellowing from one end of the room to the other through efficient-looking telephones. Bedlam, in comparison, would have been heaven. Through it all the incessant tapping of typewriters and the perpetual buzz of telephone bells, gave a tenor to the bass-toned roar filling the main office until even Storm and Grimm began to feel thick-headed.

Their escort banged on a door marked:

Geo. Warren – Chief Ed.

and flung it open before the last knock stopped echoing. All three were halfway in the room when the Chief Editor glared up from one telephone and jerked the receiver off another.

Swarthy, unshaven for at least two days, beetle-browed, the massive Chief Editor of the hottest tabloid paper in New York was rasping into the telephone a series of cannon-ball orders which streamed with fluent profanity.

He finished with one telephone and rapped 'keep it' into the other before swerving round on the newcomers.

'Yep?'

Their escort pointed unnecessarily to Storm and Grimm.

'Dem boxing guys, Boss.'

Warren just glared ferociously at the Englishmen, then smiled with sudden and surprising geniality. He pressed a button on his switchboard.

'Keep all my calls,' he rapped.

As the Chief Editor pushed the telephone away from him, cleared a mass of papers, and, with a celerity telling of long practice, revealed a bottle, three glasses and a box of powerful-looking cigars, he leaned back and spoke with the soft intonation of a Southern burr:

'Sit down, gentlemen. Cigars, or smoke your own dope. Drink's comin'. What kin I do for you?'

Storm sat down obediently.

'I don't know – yet,' he admitted cautiously.

Warren began pouring drinks.

'Well, maybe it's that li'l story we wrote up, Mr Storm. I jus' can't tell you how sorry I am, an' that's the real truth. The guy that wrote that story's getting the biggest takedown he's ever had since his lullaby days, and it won't be my fault if he doesn't write up a full apology! Take it from me he's –'

Storm grinned.

'I'm not worrying about that write-up. It's the little job that followed it I'm after.'

Warren's squat body went taut as he glared up.

'What job?'

Leaning back in his chair, Storm flicked a speck of ash from his perfectly creased trousers.

He said gently: 'You can tell the bright lad who wrote up that pack of lics that we meant all we said and a lot more! Tell him that all the gangsters in the universe wouldn't make us turn a hair! Tell him we've been telephoning the British Ambassador at Washington and that he's kicking up the biggest shindy U.S.A.'s ever thought of! Tell him – ' He leaned forward, tapping the gaping Warren's fleshy shoulder. 'Tell him to put more lies in his write-up than he's ever thought of in his young life, and get you to help him! That ought to do the trick!'

Warren shot him a look of almost panic from beneath his beetling brows.

'What trick?'

Storm grinned engagingly and stretched his legs. There was considerable satisfaction in having tied up the great George Warren, Chief Editor, but too much leg-pull would have made him lose sight of his main objective – that of finding, if possible, why O'Halloran was hostile and who were the likely gunmen behind the outrage of the afternoon. Warren, if he had realised the crazy plan of reprisals formulating in Storm's mind would have gulped: 'Heck!

What innocents!' Neither of the Englishmen had the slightest idea of the deep-rooted fear inspired by the gangster menace, nor of the soulless murder-machinery run by rival racketeers.

'I've just been talking to a lad called O'Halloran at Police Headquarters,' said Storm mildly. 'I don't like O'Halloran and I don't like the way he froze up on that Long Island shooting job this morning.'

Warren's thick lips closed in a straight line. He lost his uncertainty and from his prominent eyes there shone a kind of secondhand but biting fear. His voice was thick.

'Were you in that car?'

'We were,' assented Storm grimly, and showed the hole in his hat.

Warren seemed frozen stiff. Then:

'And you got away with it! Cripes, but you're lucky!'

'O'Halloran suggested that,' murmured Storm.

Warren hardly seemed to hear him. He was staring through, not at, the two Englishmen, and that frightening expression of near-fear sent an irrepressible shiver through their blood.

'That's Redhead!' he rasped hoarsely. 'Only Redhead would have done it! And I thought he was out of the country or I'd 'a cut my fingers off before okaying that story!'

'Nice of you,' Storm murmured, 'but what's it all about? Who's Redhead?'

'He's the deadliest swine we've ever had to contend with. He's got more murders against him than all the others put together. There ain't a racket he's not in somewhere, and there ain't a fly cop can pull him for selling poison liquor. I reckoned he was out of the States, Storm, or I swear I wouldn't have run that story. We've had it before. Dumb guys grinning at the gangs – and it's usually their last grin when Redhead's near. He thinks he's Almighty, and, tarnation, he damn near is!'

There was something compelling about Warren's manner, making Storm and Grimm realise that the newspaper man was giving them the naked truth. To them, imbued with the Englishman's unshakable belief in the superiority of law and order, it seemed impossible. But they were in New York, not London, and the grip of the gangs was tightening round them, monstrous, murderous, filling the very air with ominous threats.

'So that's it, is it? We trod on Redhead's corns and he's after us. And all the police in New York daren't – '

'It ain't daren't!' interrupted Warren, taking a grip on himself. 'It's can't. They think it's him, but they can't be sure – and if they were they wouldn't know who it was, apart from just the name: Redhead. That's all you can get from squealers with the gangs, just Redhead, and it's enough to make a man order his box if Redhead's put him on the spot.' He crashed one great hand into a vast palm. 'I reckon O'Halloran thought you'd really said all those things, Storm, and a man who'd do that asks for trouble. I reckon he wants to get you out of the country fast, because if anything happened to you there'd be a stink with your little island, and we don't want that in U.S.A.'

He pushed back his chair and stood up, pointing the tip of his cigar towards Storm.

'Son, you don't know things over here. You don't know Redhead, and I reckon you want a peck at him. Well, forget it! I wouldn't print your story for all the gold in China! It'd sign your death warrant. Swallow your pride and get out of here while you can. Don't go first class. Travel third, like a couple of bohunks, and don't show your noses out on the first class deck until you've reached Cherbourg.'

He shot out a hand, gripping Storm's.

'Say! I could shoot myself for printing that story, but I'm right glad to've seen ye both. But the yarn went round that Redhead was halfway across the Atlantic, and things were kinda dull. I'm darn sorry. I'll print a headliner, saying it was all bunk, though if Redhead's after you a headliner won't help. I'll put a coupla men to keep an eye on you, and I reckon O'Halloran's watching, too.'

He looked sombre.

'And don't argue, you guys. Believe me, if you don't get out damn quick you'll be stone cold in no time at all, and I kinda don't want your shooting up on my conscience, see? Come an' see us again, when things are quieter. All right? G'bye.'

2

A LITTLE DISPLAY OF STRENGTH

At the doors of *The Courier* offices Storm and Grimm were annoyed to find the heavily-built, blonde figure of O'Halloran standing at the door of a solidly-built saloon car.

After a brief but one-sided conversation the Englishmen clambered dutifully inside. Warren had been right. The authorities of New York were making as sure as humanly possible that no 'accident' stopped them from getting safely back to their native land. The two men felt stunned that such precautions were being taken; the deadly danger in which they stood, now that they were definitely put on the spot by the deadly Redhead, struck more forcefully through the hush-hush actions of the police than through the attack on the Long Island Road.

There followed a brief but explanatory talk with a worthy who stood on the dizzy heights of New York officialdom. While the city presented its profoundest regrets to two such splendid sportsmen, at the same time it must be impressed on them that they had incurred the enmity of a powerful member of the criminal classes. The high official had instructions to smuggle them out of the country immediately. The affair was most unfortunate, but only by such a move could their safety and the good name of New York City be maintained.

The next ship, they were assured, was the *Hoveric*, due to sail early next morning and as a safety measure the authorities had already booked two third-class steerage berths under assumed names. The authorities would watch Mr Storm and Mr Grimm very closely, but they were earnestly requested to keep out of sight as much as possible. The Captain of the *Hoveric* had instructions to keep a close watch over his two very important passengers.

'So that's that,' said Storm, when they were left alone in the room of their hotel. 'It's no use kicking, Roger. But I'd like to have a little private interview with Redhead. To think we've got to suffer steerage from here to Cherbourg!'

As with all things, the sufferings passed however, though leaving a deep-seated hostility to the unseen, unknown Redhead.

To have rebelled against the official decree would have been impossible. The remorseless arm of the United States' Authorities had closed down on them, and they did what they were told, willy-nilly. But their helplessness and the overpowering sense of impotency made them chafe. In the words of Storm, as they deserted the *Hoveric* at Cherbourg and returned ten minutes later as first-class passengers:

'I'd like to have a shot at Redhead one of these fine days. I only wish the devil would come to England. I'd show him!'

Which utterance, though he knew it not, was more than prophetic.

Sunning themselves on the sports deck, Martin Storm and Roger Grimm recovered quickly from the discomfort of their enforced journey by steerage. Idly they watched Ginger at his fancy tricks, the flaming red of his hair being a strong point against him.

'What's he up to now?' Grimm queried.

'Ask me,' retorted Storm vulgarly.

While the cousins were in ignorance of the next display of strength everyone else on deck seemed to know what to expect.

From the small, and in the main, admiring crowd which had gathered round Ginger one worthy, gloriously bedecked in a suit of loud plus fours, swaggered to the chalk line drawn by an attendant steward. Raising his arms in the time-honoured fashion of prize fighters he grinned expectantly towards Ginger.

Storm gave a snort.

'I didn't know Tiger Norse was travelling, or I'd have caught the next boat.'

'You wouldn't have caught anything of the kind,' retorted Grimm mildly, staring at the pugilist and the waiting Ginger.

They knew Tiger Norse as a professional, and as poor a specimen as had ever left England.

The antagonists, both men of exceptional muscular development and both obviously kow-towing to popular approval, were grasping each other with the right hand above the right wrist. Locked in this fashion they began a strong but showy struggle, each striving to pull his opponent's left foot over the thin white line.

'Revolting,' murmured Storm.

'Disgusting,' avowed Grimm.

Nevertheless both men found it difficult to take their eyes from the combatants. Tiger Norse, with his training and seven years' experience in boxing camps, should have found it a cake-walk; but the veins showed blue against his swarthy forehead as he pulled, and small beads of sweat decorated his battered face. Ginger, on the other hand, was smiling a superior and altogether objectionable smile. Beneath his thin tennis shirt the fine, rippling muscles of his shoulders moved easily. Tiger was puny in comparison.

Again Storm admitted to himself that Ginger, for all his distasteful love of popularity, not only desired but demanded respect.

Storm and Grimm found themselves staring fascinatedly at the display of brute strength. They felt the same pull as they would have done at a Test Match, experienced the same inability to think of personalities in the tenseness of the struggle.

Slowly, inexorably, Tiger Norse's right foot slid forward until it first touched, then crossed, the white line. Almost spontaneously a burst of clapping came from the crowd of spectators, with an extra exuberance from the delightful-looking occupant of a deck-chair immediately in front of the cousins.

Storm looked at her with interest. By no means a Don Juan, he was highly susceptible to feminine charms, and the girl in the deck-chair was streets ahead of anything else on view.

He could see her profile clearly, for she was leaning forward in her chair, and the glowing animation of her face made him realise with a mental frown that she was well and truly under the magnetic spell of Ginger. For a moment she looked away from the main crowd so that Storm and Grimm had a perfect full-face view.

It was a face, Storm considered, which would not have suffered in comparison with the most polished star of Elstree and Hollywood. He had time to see that her eyes were blue and her hair almost raven black.

Martin Storm's hostility towards the redheaded braggart who was moving blithely towards the girl developed into a keen, urgent desire to punch him on the nose.

Storm's emotions were such that when he spoke he forgot to keep his voice low.

'More than anything else in the world,' he said, 'I'd like to take the rise out of that kudos-collector.'

'So would I,' agreed Grimm, and then stared curiously at his cousin. There had been an asperity about that loudly expressed desire much deeper than Grimm saw any reason for. 'Anything up?' he demanded.

But Storm had no opportunity to reply before a man who had been lounging a few yards away, turned to them impassively. He was pleasant enough, perhaps five or six years younger than Storm, who was thirty, but his well-cut features were, at the moment, darkened by a frown. Storm had an idea that he had seen him before.

'I wish to heaven,' he said almost desperately, 'that you'd do just that!'

In common with all well-bred Englishmen Martin Storm had a genial liking for putting the next man at his ease. He did not, therefore, show his surprise. The thought, for some reason an unpleasant one, that the sturdy youth was an unlucky swain of the girl's passed through his mind as he answered cheerfully:

'Well, one never knows. Ginger's certainly asking for it.'

The stranger smiled.

'Ginger certainly cuts him down a bit. Let's hope the brute hears it.'

'Touchy, eh?' queried Storm.

'That's putting it mildly,' asserted the other, in the ready tone of one who had been bottling up a dislike of Ginger throughout the trip.

'We only joined up at Cherbourg,' Grimm informed him. 'It looks as if we missed most of the fun.'

'If you can call it fun,' grimaced the newcomer. 'Up here, on the proms, any damn place in this rotten ship, Wenlock's been lording it like a tuppenny royalty! And the trouble is that Letty – '

He broke off suddenly. Storm, who was eyeing him keenly saw that what he had mistaken for familiarity in the young man's face was, in fact, a likeness to the girl of the deck-chair.

'Might as well spill it,' he said cheerfully.

The other laughed, with an air of gratitude at having been helped out of an awkward situation.

'Ah well, you see, Letty is my sister – my name's Granville by the way, Frank Granville – and I'm pretty well convinced that Wenlock's got her thoroughly under his thumb. He's made a dead set at her ever since we left New York.' He rubbed his chin ruefully. 'Of course, Letty's affairs aren't mine, but I've taken such a dislike to Wenlock that I'd give a lot to see him pushed out of the limelight.'

Storm chuckled, finding an echo in Grimm.

'Admirable sentiments. By the way' – the question came naturally enough but Grimm knew that it had been manoeuvred and grinned to himself – 'Letty is the girl in the deck-chair, isn't she? The one Ginger is talking to?'

Frank Granville's frown returned.

'Yes. She couldn't make it more obvious if she stood on a funnel and bellowed through a megaphone.'

Storm tossed a half-smoked cigarette into the sea and watched it sink. Then:

'So Ginger doesn't like being called Ginger. And, I gather, no one's able to pull him over the white line?'

'No,' admitted Granville glumly, but with a sidelong look at Storm's massive physique. 'He staged a competition, and Norse was the other finalist. You saw how it ended up.'

'Sure,' murmured Storm, suspiciously mild. 'I saw. Now, what about sloping back to the rails where you were. I don't think anyone's seen us talking, do you? Ginger or your sister I mean? Good. Then get back and answer anything I ask as loudly as you like.' He winked jubilantly. 'We're going to have fun.'

'And the game?' demanded Grimm, as Granville acted on Storm's instructions.

'Unless I'm seriously miscalculating,' grinned Storm, 'I'm about to give Ginger a surprise packet and earn a certain amount of unspoken abuse.'

He winked at the eagerly watching Granville as, with a sudden, cavernous yawn he stretched his massive frame until the chair creaked.

'Hey-ho, Roger! Boring kind of life, this. Pity we didn't join the ship at New York.'

'Why's that?' demanded Grimm, following his cue and speaking well above normal.

'We could have played some little games,' continued Storm, as though taking the whole ship into his confidence and expecting the passengers to weep in sympathy. 'I wouldn't have minded a shot at that ginger fellow.'

He was gazing through half-closed eyes at Wenlock, who was talking animatedly to Letty Granville. As the 'ginger' came out, rolled appreciatively round Storm's tongue, Wenlock suddenly went red, a good, deep, beetroot red. He looked up, breaking heedlessly across a sentence from the girl, and Storm saw a glint of fury in his green eyes.

Storm chuckled inwardly. The fish was rising to the bait. He stretched again.

'Ah, well! It's too late now, I suppose. I notice he hopped away pretty soon after the battle. Wonder who he was? You don't know him, do you, Roger?'

Grimm shook his head.

'No, and I'm not sorry,' he supported manfully.

Neither of them was looking towards Wenlock, who rose slowly to his feet and moved towards them. Fifty pairs of eyes were fixed on Storm.

He had staged an outrageous breach of good manners, but a sizeable sprinkling of the passengers felt sympathetic; Wenlock had made a number of very bad friends during the voyage. Tensely they wondered now what would happen.

Storm and Grimm alone seemed oblivious of Wenlock's cat-footed approach. The former waved a cheery hand at Frank Granville as his deep voice boomed out.

'Who was the ginger cove, sonny? Any idea?'

Someone grabbed Storm's arm.

His expression, carefully schooled to a look of natural surprise, met Wenlock's furious stare. A few shrewd spectators wondered whether it was all quite as accidental as it appeared to be.

'I hope you weren't talking of me,' Wenlock said softly.

His eyes held a devilish vindictiveness, and under their glare Storm lost a little of the carefree exuberance with which he had started on the mild adventure. They were the eyes of a man not only heartless but soulless, and the realisation sent a cold thrill along Storm's spine. Then:

'Well I'm jiggered!' he gasped. 'I thought you'd gone to your cabin.'

Wenlock's queer eyes blazed, but he kept his fury well in hand.

'Perhaps you will apologise, Mr – '

'Smith,' supplied Storm untruthfully. Then ingenuously: 'Apologise? What for?'

For a moment he thought Wenlock would strike out, but before the other spoke again he grinned understandingly.

'Oh, I've got you. Of course. Well, look here. Let's have one of those little tug-o'-war games, and if you win I'll bend the knee and if I do we'll call it quits. Is it on?'

Wenlock's lips set in a surly line as he stepped back a foot. From half-a-dozen points along the deck came titters of amusement. Storm knew perfectly well that he had his man in a cleft stick. No matter how outrageously he had insulted the other, the fair and square offer to make amends gave the red-haired man no choice but to accept. But in accepting he was anything but gracious.

'I suppose I'll have to,' he said grudgingly.

Storm beamed as blandly as ever. If Wenlock had taken the offer sportingly he would have felt more than a bit sheepish; after all, the calculated insult was enough to make any man wild. But there was something in Wenlock, something in the hard, ruthless expression which made him determined to go on with it.

Wenlock, already halfway to the chalked line, spoke over his shoulder.

'Let's get the business over.'

The pro-Wenlock element felt a little disgruntled. The least their hero could have done was to have offered time whilst the unorthodox challenger changed into rubber shoes.

In spite of Storm's earlier ill-mannered attack the challenger was gaining adherents. There was an infectious buoyancy about his genial good-humour which made it difficult to dislike him. The interest in the struggle between Tiger Norse and Wenlock had been mild compared with the tension which seemed to fill the very hearts of the passengers on the sports deck, and soon others came hurrying to the scene.

Storm slipped his coat off, throwing it lightly to Roger Grimm before squaring up to his opponent. A volunteer referee murmured: 'Back an inch, Mr Wenlock, please,' and the two men grasped each other's wrists.

Almost before they had gripped Storm felt a fierce tug and was dragged remorselessly forward by a colossal heave which it seemed impossible to resist. In a flash he was within an inch of the white line, dragged by that first calculated heave. But he was in much better training than Tiger Norse, and the split second gave him time to set his muscles. Without changing the mildly amused expression of his rugged face he threw all he knew into keeping on the right side of the line. Wenlock might have been pulling against the side of the *Hoveric* itself for all the impression he made.

Still smiling, Storm saw the change in the other's manner. Probably for the first time since he had boarded the ship Wenlock was up against an opponent whose strength matched his own. He was taking it badly, and the spectators were beginning to show a certain restiveness and disappointment at this lack of sportsmanship.

Storm maintained his pressure, sliding his foot back inch by inch until he had regained his lost ground. Fraction by fraction he dragged his man forward. He saw the sweat rising from Wenlock's forehead and felt a dampness about his own.

As the seconds dragged into minutes and they strained against each other like great bulls, he knew that Wenlock was weakening.

Throwing every ounce of strength that he had into the long drawn-out effort, Storm leaned backwards, dragging his man remorselessly forward. He was staring into those glowing green eyes when something jabbed sharply into his forearm. Glancing down he saw the white nail of Wenlock's thumb breaking into his flesh.

He grunted, swearing beneath his breath. He could lose with any man, but foul play enraged him. Once – twice – thrice! He pulled sensing the unspoken, overwhelming hatred of his antagonist.

Wenlock slipped forward an inch. His bones cracked and his muscles rippled as he pulled, but that relentless strength gripping his wrist and dragging him remorselessly forward could not be denied. With the third pull he stumbled into defeat.

Storm steadied him before letting him go, and as he stretched his arms with relief grinned cheerfully.

'Mine, I think. Thanks.'

Wenlock said nothing, but his green eyes burned with a fire which sent a chill through Storm's veins. Beetroot red, the loser swung away, looking neither right nor left nor sparing a word even for the expressionless Letty Granville as he made for the cabins. Storm's eyes hardened for a moment before he shrugged his shoulders and turned to Roger Grimm.

'A nasty cove, Roger, but we've taken the rise out of him. Where's my coat?'

'It wouldn't surprise me,' said Grimm as he helped the other into his jacket, 'to hear more about it.'

'Nor me,' agreed Storm.

And for a second time the cousins had been unwittingly prophetic. The evil spirit of Wenlock was hovering about them, and the air was thick with coming thunder.

3

STARTLING DEVELOPMENTS

The introduction which Frank Granville – very quickly 'Granny' to Storm and Grimm – effected between the cousins and his sister Letty was not a great success. Letty, in spite of her startling beauty, proved that she could be cold if not definitely unfriendly. These things worried the genial Martin not at all, for a modest bit of detective work on his part revealed the fact that her coldness to him was as nothing compared to her coldness towards Ralph Wenlock. He realised that the smashing of an idol with feet of clay was likely to bring a certain torrent of wrath on the head of the smasher, and he suffered his period of cold-shouldering amiably.

Two things perturbed him in some measure, the first to be brushed aside, and the second to lurk at the back of his mind for several days.

After a stroll on deck with Roger Grimm he had dived below for a fresh packet of cigarettes and had seen Wenlock and Frank Granville in what appeared to be close consultation. Unwittingly he heard sufficient to gather that they were quarrelling. The whys and wherefores of the quarrel interested him not at all; it was the fact that they were talking with more than a touch of intimacy that surprised him.

The second perturbing thing was that Letty Granville appeared to be worried. The anxiety he felt over this he had the sound sense to keep to himself. But during a conversation with Granville just before Southampton was sighted he learned of a possible explanation.

A road smash, nearly five years before, had ended fatally for Sir Frank and Lady Granville, leaving their son and daughter well-provided for. Granville and his sister, putting their heads together, had decided that travel was the thing for them, and they travelled.

Storm discovered that they were now making the voyage home six months before schedule. He could understand that an unsettled homecoming might cause a certain amount of anxiety.

Later he cursed himself for not looking more deeply into Granville's occasional bursts of confidence. For the time being it was the immediate problem he found disturbing – Letty Granville in the spirit and in the flesh.

There was talk, for no ship of the size of the *Hoveric* could exist without its scandalmongers, and whispers reached his ears; that the breach between Letty and Wenlock was caused as much by Wenlock's complete disappearance from the social life on the *Hoveric* as the manner of his defeat; that she had tried to see the red-headed man in his private cabin; that she suspected her brother had had something to do with Wenlock's defeat; that Letty and Frank were bad friends in consequence.

'Reduces me to a nervous wreck,' grumbled Storm on the last night, as Roger Grimm slipped into a pair of gaily-striped pyjamas. 'I mean, what did she ever see in him? It didn't take *me* three seconds to recognise a cad and a bounder!'

'Do shut up,' grumbled Grimm. 'Sleep it off, old chap, and turn that light out.'

Little or nothing was seen of Wenlock the next morning. He was, Storm learned, the son of a wealthy American, his complete lack of American accent was explained by the fact that he had been educated at Eton and Oxford, and he was on a trip to England on his father's business interests. The interests were vague, but Granville believed they were something in oil, and at the back of Storm's mind was a hazy recollection that the name Wenlock spelt power and money.

In keeping with his lifelong habit of taking everything with amiable philosophy, Storm was not particularly surprised when, three hours out of Southampton, a summons came from the Captain's cabin. Would Mr Storm and Mr Grimm be good enough to visit Captain Roker?

The cousins had been packing for the past hour and had seen nothing of the raking grey ship drawn up alongside the mountainous *Hoveric* and from which a Very Important Personage had crossed the intervening stretch of water on a motor launch flying the blue ensign. Meeting him in Captain Roker's cabin, Storm, after a moment's uncertain racking of memory, recognised him to be a prominent M.P.

The Personage greeted them pleasantly enough, adding: 'I'm sorry that my call is an official one.' He smiled. 'They tell me that you've been causing some anxiety in the United States.'

'Oi!' broke in Storm, gasping at the fact that the shindy in New York was looked on so seriously that the Assistant to the Home Secretary and Prime Minister should seek a personal interview. What the deuce was coming? He grimaced to himself but went on naturally enough: 'Not of our making, I assure you.'

The Personage smiled dryly.

'Whichever way it was, gentlemen, I'm afraid it has caused a considerable stir with the authorities in New York. The chief apprehension is, to give you a partial explanation which you certainly deserve, that the man called – er – '

'Redhead,' supplied Storm affably.

'That is the man,' agreed the Personage, relieved to have the undignified nickname taken out of his mouth. 'He is rather more than the usual type of gangster. In fact – ' The emissary from the Home Secretary broke off, gazing keenly and seriously at the two large young men who sat at ease before him. When he spoke again his voice was measured and sobered by the fear which had so marked the New York authorities. The sinister influence of the unseen, unknown Redhead seemed to lurk in the small cabin, and the air was chill.

'In fact,' he went on soberly, 'we have every reason to fear that this man – '

'Redhead,' interposed Storm helpfully.

'Is,' went on the Assistant imperturbably, 'bent on executing a grave and very large criminal coup. We have every reason to believe that this individual will operate not only in the United States but also in Europe and – er – most likely in England. In view of that, gentlemen' – the speaker's voice deepened – 'the need, the absolute *necessity* for complete silence on all matters which so unfortunately concerned you while in New York cannot be too strongly emphasised.'

He paused again, and it struck Storm that he was at once reluctant and embarrassed, which meant that something of a climax was coming. Slowly:

'You will have to forgive me for this, gentlemen, but I – er – I have been instructed to advise you that the matter is viewed by the Home Secretary as one of such vital importance that any information which might be divulged by you on the matter of – er – Redhead, will not only be an indictable offence but will be sufficient to give grounds for instant detention at His Majesty's Government's discretion.'

The Assistant Secretary stopped. He was frankly concerned with the probability of their rebellious reception of his ultimatum. It had been an unorthodox and an unpleasant task and he was glad to be at the end of it.

Consequently, relief tempered his amazement at the sight of Martin Storm's rugged face splitting, in company with Roger Grimm's, from an expression of lugubrious bewilderment to one of explosive mirth.

'Good lord, Roger! What about that? Indictable offence – immediate detention – state secrets!'

Across the faces of the Assistant Secretary and Captain Roker a first mystified and then comprehending grin appeared.

The Assistant Secretary allowed them a full thirty seconds before making a tentative interruption.

'So I may take it, gentlemen, that you will have no hesitation in acting on the – er – instructions of the – er – Home Office?'

Storm, almost recovered, extended a genial hand.

'Sir,' he said solemnly, 'you may rely on our absolute discretion. Not a word of our adventures on foreign soil shall be breathed to a soul. You agree, Roger?'

'Absolutely,' asserted Roger Grimm firmly.

For the next two hours Storm and Grimm wandered about the *Hoveric* in a state of barely suppressed merriment. But Granville, who tried hard to solve the mystery, got nothing further than:

'Granny, old son, the Captain told us a funny story! Oh, my hat! My sides!'

Southampton came at last. The *Hoveric* berthed with that stately, breathless exactitude of position after manoeuvres which sent the hearts of the uninitiated into panicky fears of collision against the harbour walls. Storm and Grimm, comparatively sober and secure in the knowledge that Letty Granville had echoed, howbeit not so warmly, her brother's invitation for them to spend a week or longer at Ledsholm Grange, their home in Sussex.

'Funny if someone started potting us, wouldn't it?' murmured Storm as he and his cousin viewed the ever-shifting crowds lining the docks, the bawling porters, hysterical relatives and staccato-voiced officials with the deep satisfaction peculiar to the returning traveller.

The next moment he felt himself suddenly lifted off his feet by a human avalanche stampeding towards the deep, muddy waters of the harbour. Grimm, a yard nearer the edge than Storm, grabbed at a stanchion and heaved backwards for all he was worth, bawling like a madman.

'Get back, curse you, get back! Do you all want to be drowned like rats? Get back!'

He heaved like a superman, with Storm, on his feet in a trice, following suit against the second stanchion and forming a cordon with the help of a handful of men quick enough on the uptake to realise the calamitous outcome of the panic if the crowd toppled over to the sea. The cordon of flesh and bone bent and swayed beneath the mad onslaught, but with the stanchions which were placed at intervals along the quayside giving them support they kept the shrieking, bellowing crowd at bay. Gradually the ghastly danger struck home to the panickers, and the pressure eased. Shouts grew less frequent and less hysterical, white, strained faces turned towards the sea.

Why it had started, what had caused the maniacal stampede which might have proved a ghastly massacre of innocents was for the moment totally beyond Storm's comprehension. He caught Grimm's eye as he moved quickly away from the spot.

'Hump,' grunted Grimm. 'I wonder – oh, damn!'

He snatched his hand from a wooden stanchion, staring down on it for a moment in stupefaction. From the middle of the index finger of his right hand a small stream of blood began to flow.

Storm saw it and his mouth tightened.

'That's rifle fire,' he said tersely. 'Who the –'

He broke off, grabbing at his hat as it was lifted from his head as though by a heavy gust of wind. Through the crown was a small, clean hole. His eyes lost every expression save one of hard, unflinching purpose as he stared upwards to the towering deck of the *Hoveric*.

For a split second he saw the gleam of something long and bright almost directly above them, a wide-brimmed hat, and beneath it a glimpse of a man's face staring down at him.

In spite of the distance, he knew his man!

Ralph Wenlock! There wasn't a shadow of doubt. Ginger had started his reprisals and started them quickly, with all the murderous intent which Storm had seen in the glowing green eyes and hard, merciless features.

For perhaps ten seconds Storm stood on the edge of the quay, staring upwards.

Wenlock's move had been devilishly cunning. Waiting until the majority of the *Hoveric's* passengers had disembarked he had gone to the top deck where he was hidden from the sight of everyone apart from a chance sailor, and had taken aim at the cousins with a cold-bloodedness worthy of the blackest hearted Chicago gangster. The almost insane lust for vengeance was incredible; Storm wondered coolly what else was behind the attack.

With a grimace at Grimm, Storm turned his thoughts towards the stampede. Was there any connection between the disturbance and the shooting?

He let the idea go, as being too fantastic for words. The stampede had merely given Wenlock good cover and lessened the chances of failure to escape.

Storm knew that the day of reckoning with the ginger-haired American was yet to come.

The cousins had the choice of two things and they discussed them quietly as they made their way towards the Customs House. They could report the shooting to the police, or they could keep quiet and let Ginger fancy that he had been unrecognised. Finally they decided on a middle course, that of reporting it without giving a description of Wenlock. Thus, said Storm, they would ease their conscience and Wenlock's mind at the same time.

Grimm's retort was neither courteous nor complimentary.

Storm cocked an eye at the thinning crowd.

'I don't think there's much chance of reporters button-holing us now, old boy. Let's have a look at the source of the trouble.'

Staring towards one spot round which a heaving throng of spectators still surged he saw the helmets of a dozen policemen and the peak caps of several officials.

'There we are,' he said easily as they moved towards the crowd. 'Mad dog, probably, or someone suffering from sunstroke. Shift your lazy bones.'

Grimm shifted, keeping his injured hand in his pocket. They approached the crowd with unusual sobriety, having, in the words of Storm, had quite enough shindy for one day.

Their height enabled them to see the trouble above the heads of the lesser humans, and again Storm wondered whether the trouble had been quite so accidental as they might have imagined.

It seemed that the dock trolleys had crashed head-first. Several people were being attended by first-aid men, and from the remarks which floated from still excited travellers they gathered that a number had been taken to hospital.

Then from the lips of a white-bearded patriarch they heard the word 'guns'.

Storm's eyes narrowed as he approached and inquired for information. The white-bearded patriarch came well up to scratch.

'A most amazing occurrence, sir! An outrage! A matter for the severest disciplinary measure! I have never – '

'Couple of drivers went blotto, eh?' queried Storm, playing for quick results.

An indignant and furious glance was flung in his direction.

'It had nothing to do with drivers, sir! The Royal Mail has been stolen! All the post on board the *Hoveric* has been stolen by armed bandits! And the unutterable scoundrels shot down officials and sent these two trolleys crashing against each other to prevent pursuit!'

'Any captures?' demanded Storm quickly.

The aged one shook his head.

'None at all! All three men escaped! And but for the activities of a number of heroic young men along the quayside there would have been a still further tragedy. I shudder to think of what might have happened; but luckily, sir, there still exist men of whom England may well be proud. In spite of the panic, in spite of the veritable stampede, they stood with their backs to the wall.'

Storm slid gracefully out of the crush towards the customs shed, with Grimm in close attendance.

'Hear that, Roger? Three men with guns pinched the mail bags and sheered off. They must have had a car.' He scratched his head thoughtfully. 'Lot of guns about today, aren't there?'

'A lot too many,' snorted Grimm. 'It's nearly as bad as New York, Martin, what with guns and what with Redhead – '

Storm went suddenly still.

'My God!' he burst out. 'Ginger – Redhead! Get that, chew that! Think about it! Ginger – Redhead! Redhead was coming to England, they fancied, and Ginger's here. Ginger shot at us with his little gun and I don't believe he would have done it because of the tussle we had the other day. Oh, boy! Can Ginger be Redhead? And if he is, aren't we going to have something to say about it?'

4

THE DEPARTMENT
WITHOUT NAMES

Sir William Divot was a much worried and harassed politician who combined a frigid manner with a warm heart and a genial if limited sense of humour. Not for many months had he laughed so heartily nor chuckled so deeply at frequent intervals. But by the time the train ran into Waterloo Sir William had thoroughly immersed himself in a welter of facts, figures and fancies, and he forgot the lumbering, genial Martin Storm and his less forceful but equally pleasant companion. Muttering an apology as he trod on the toes of the detective who was making sure that no harm befell such an important member of the Government, he walked hurriedly towards the waiting Daimler saloon, and instructed his chauffeur to make for Whitehall.

He was thinking of bandits, although the very word was anathema. Bandits in England. Pah! The thing was outrageous. Where was Scotland Yard? Why was the special department at Whitehall called in? Anyone would think the very country was overrun with armed robbers.

Knowing nothing of the outrage at the docks and the theft of the *Hoveric's* mail, he appreciated that the figures whirling in his head, figures telling of the increasing number of post office hold-ups and armed robberies, were impressive. But he secretly believed that there was a great deal of exaggeration in the business, and he was firmly convinced that the talk he had heard of the American gangster, Redhead, was distorted out of all proportion.

His chauffeur, a young and personable servitor, was keenly disappointed. Whitehall meant work, probably for the rest of the evening, and there was a certain bright-eyed little lady at the *Hotel Clarion* who was at that moment bedecking herself in anticipation of an evening out.

But Sir William knew nothing of these things and in any case had vitally important matters of state to attend. Stepping from the Daimler he told his servitor to get himself some tea.

'I don't know how long I'll be, Perret. But be back within half-an-hour.'

Sir William, entering the gloomy portals of the Home Office, nodded absently to several commissionaires and walked steadily on, his mind reeling with those facts, figures and fancies concerning bandit outrages and their total loss to the community. Gad! If the figures were right nearly half a million pounds worth of valuables had been stolen within the past three months. Colossal!

His journey was neither straightforward nor short, but he knew his way perfectly and after five minutes stopped outside a drab-looking door doing its best to hide its insignificant existence. Sharply he tapped an apparently haphazard but actually prearranged tattoo on the dingy oak surface. The door slid open. He stepped over the threshold, hearing the door slide back into position with the start of apprehension which he always felt when reaching 'Z' Department – more often known as Department Z.

The Assistant Secretary was one of the few men who knew the name of Number One of 'Z' Department. Gordon Craigie, hatchet-faced, monosyllabic, smoker of a potent smelling meerschaum was Whitehall's nearest approach to a mystery man.

As Chief of 'Z' Department he carried onerous and inordinately difficult work out with considerable success and it could be said with some certainty that he – helped by his courageous band of agents – did more than any man in the world to prevent war rising from the little flames of insurrection simmering in the hole-in-the-corner principalities throughout Europe and the Near East.

But 'Z' Department did not confine itself to international problems. It was closely linked with Scotland Yard although only the Chief Commissioner and a very select band of C.I.D. officials knew it. The matter on which Sir William Divot called concerned both home activities and the United States.

Craigie was sitting at a large, flat-topped desk smoking his inevitable meerschaum. His finger moved from the electric button which operated the sliding door as his thin lips parted in greeting.

'Hallo, Divot. Glad to see you. What's the trouble?'

Sir William's lips parted a little petulantly.

'It's this Redhead business, Craigie. Are you sure it isn't being overdone?'

Craigie's meerschaum left his lips rather abruptly.

'What put that into your head? I suppose you've just seen Storm and the other fellow.'

Mention of the genial giant brought a reflective smile to Sir William's shrewd eyes.

'Yes – Yes! A most – er – engaging young man, Craigie. Most engaging and most – er – tractable.'

'Hump,' muttered Craigie, who knew a great deal more about Martin Storm and Roger Grimm than Sir William dreamed.

'I hadn't the slightest difficulty with him,' went on Sir William, obviously resentful of that 'hump'. 'You needn't worry about that. However, the Prime Minister wants information on the Redhead affair. I suppose you have a report.'

'I've sent it through to your office. But don't think because we don't know much about Redhead that he's a myth. He isn't. I'd rather call him the Devil!'

Sir William eyed him uncertainly. There was a grimness about Craigie's manner which carried conviction.

'Well – you're looking after it, aren't you?'

Craigie heaved a sigh and refilled his pipe. Then:

'I don't want to, Divot, but I'm going to unburden myself. It's all in the report, but it'll probably hit you harder if I talk about it. Now listen. Redhead is in England. I don't think there's a shadow of doubt about that. But we haven't found out what it is that he's after. There seems to be a connection between him and this series of outrages, but there's an important point to remember. None of the attacks has ended fatally. The hold-ups have always fallen short of murder, and Redhead is a killer if he's nothing else.'

'A man with any intelligence,' deposed Sir William portentiously, 'would appreciate and allow for the difference between American and English laws.'

'Tell that to Aunt Sally!' snorted Craigie. 'Divot, if Redhead reaches the stage he's reached in America we'll have a hell of a time before we get rid of him! I know you don't like strong language, but you don't know Redhead. He's foul, and he's a killer. He's after something big in

England and when he gets going properly nothing short of a heavy armed force will deter him, and then we'll be lucky if we can strike before he's got what he wants and gone! You don't believe it? Well, slip down to the American Embassy and ask what they think of him there!'

Much to the relief of his chauffeur Sir William did not slip down to the American Embassy, but he spent ten minutes at Number 10, Downing Street before Perret was able to keep his date with the little girl at the *Clarion*.

Meanwhile Gordon Craigie, still ruffled after his rare outburst, was speaking to three keen-eyed, capable-looking young men. The young men were members of the little-known 'Z' Department. There were times when they would drop out for a week, a month or two, reappearing without warning or explanation; that was the bright side of the Department. The black side concerned those who went but never returned, and there were many disappearances which had no explanation outside the walls of Craigie's office.

When death calls to those in the Secret Service it leaves no obituary.

None of the three men in his office was addressed by name during the interview; it was exceptional that Craigie saw them at once. Oft times agents, in their off periods, would drink from the same bottles at the same night clubs without knowing that their opposite numbers were members of the Department. The one Masonic sign was used only in extreme emergency.

'Number Seven,' said Craigie thoughtfully, 'you pick up young Wenlock. I'm not at all sure that he is the dutiful son of his father that he's made out to be. Pick him up at the *Clarion*, where Number Ten's keeping an eye on him until you get there. Don't let him out of your sight – better take your Frazer-Nash with you in case he moves suddenly. All right?'

Craigie pressed the button and the sliding door opened and closed before he spoke again.

'Number Eight – you've lost Zoeman, haven't you?'

''Fraid so,' admitted Number Eight ruefully. He had been put on the trail of a possible key man in the bandit game, and had lost him.

Number Eight was a lively looking worthy who could spin a cricket ball better than any man on earth. He had turned down a trip to the Antipodes for 'business reasons'.

'You can take it from me,' he said emphatically, 'that Zoeman's in it up to the neck. I don't know where he's working from but the organisation's perfect. I'd say he was working with old hands from the other side if he wasn't so careful not to shoot to kill.'

'I'm keeping that in mind,' admitted Craigie. 'He worked for Wenlock Oils up to a year ago. Maybe there's a line there. I've heard rumours about young Wenlock. Anyhow, I'm sending two men to the *Éclat* lounge. You'll follow them. Work Zoeman's trail as well as you can and try to find a connection between him and Wenlock. Maybe it's a question of American brains working through an English agent.' Craigie stopped for a moment before shooting out his query: 'Ralph Wenlock is red-haired, isn't he?'

'Flamin',' Number Eight assured him. 'Think he might be the Bad Man, Chief? With Zoeman his English agent?'

'I wouldn't be surprised,' vouchsafed Craigie, guardedly.

He watched Number Eight disappear through the sliding door before turning to the remaining agent.

'Well, Number Twelve. Glad to see you back.'

'Glad to be back,' smiled Number Twelve.

'You handled that Muranian job well,' said Craigie with rare praise. 'Redhead's a bigger job, though. Learn anything on the voyage?'

'Enough to make me mighty curious,' said Number Twelve. 'You've got my report.'

'Hump,' muttered Craigie. 'Well, there's some talk of Zoeman being in the Ledsholm village area, twelve miles from Lewes. You'll find a man named Cripps, Benjamin Cripps, at the local pub, and from all accounts he's talkative.'

He stood up, his aspect that of a man of great determination and courage.

'Redhead's in the country,' he said, the words dropping from his thin lips like pieces of ice. '*We've got to get him, and we've got to get Zoeman.* Call for any help you want, and don't hang fire with even half a chance. All right?'

'So far,' grinned Number Twelve, gripping his Chief's extended hand. 'See you sometime.'

Craigie watched his sturdy figure slip through the sliding doorway and as he turned round to the empty room his hatchet face was grim and hard.

Number Twelve had followed Wenlock from America, and in his report was the story of Storm and Grimm. Letty Granville's friendship for Wenlock was also there, and the supposedly unnoticed shooting episode after the bandit hold-up on the quay.

Craigie discounted the tussle on the sports deck as being too trivial to cause attempted murder. What fool game had those idiots, Storm and Grimm, been up to?

Of course, they had fallen foul of Redhead over that boxing interview with the Press. Which suggested that Wenlock and Redhead *were* one and the same.

Craigie was not prepared to admit that they were, on the scanty evidence that he had; but things certainly pointed that way.

He grinned wryly as he refilled his meerschaum. What would the venerable leader of the Wenlock Oil Corporation say if he knew that his son was suspected of being the foulest product of the foulest era of crime in the annals of the world?

Craigie felt sorry for the old man. But he felt sorrier for Redhead's victims, and as his thoughts ran along those channels he came to the man Zoeman and his part in the English operations.

Zoeman was clever; he had escaped from one of the Department's best agents, but Craigie had an idea that he would be clever once too often.

5

OUR FRIEND THE ENEMY

Martin Storm left Grimm in the fond embraces of a crowd of relations gathered to greet him at the Philmore Crescent house of his father, Sir Joseph Grimm.

Storm himself pleaded other things and winged his way alone to a certain modest little building in Whitehall.

He and his cousin had both decided that Redhead and Wenlock were one and the same, but there had been many things brought up in their talk which needed explanation and seemed unlikely to get it. One thing and one thing only needed no further discussion and was heartily endorsed by both.

They had a large and outsize bone to pick with Wenlock. It mattered nothing at all whether he was or was not the gangster overlord who had struck fear into the heart of New York and was now trying to do the same thing to London. Their personal feud was one which, providing they lived long enough, could be settled only by themselves.

Nevertheless they had information which would be criminal to withhold from the authorities. Storm's visit to a gunsmith in Bond Street who knew him well and supplied him gladly with two automatics and a plentiful supply of ammunition, was followed by one to Whitehall.

He told a stiff, austere-looking autocrat that he wanted to see Sir William Divot.

'You have an appointment, of course?'

'I intend to see Sir William,' snapped Storm. 'Take my card in.'

The autocrat accepted the card with a stiff bow. Three minutes later his manner had considerably thawed.

'Sir William will see you, Mr Storm. This way please.'

Storm followed, smiling pleasantly as he saw the dapper little figure of Sir William Divot.

'Well, Mr Storm?'

'Not very,' said Storm, with a regrettable lapse into clownishness. 'As a matter of fact it's mere chance that I'm not a great deal worse. Look at that.'

He twirled his hat, exposing a circular hole in the crown.

Sir William stared incredulously.

'You – you – you mean that you've been fired at? You've been shot at?'

'I mean just that,' said Storm gravely. 'So was Grimm. And I can tell you, Sir William, that the boy with the gun was a man calling himself Wenlock, travelling on the *Hoveric* and supposed to be something in oil. What's more' – his face grew hard as he went on – 'Mr Wenlock, so-called, is ginger-headed!'

The Assistant Secretary's usually austere face expressed rather more than consternation.

'But – but it's outrageous! New York assured us that the man was certainly not on the *Hoveric*. They were positive! And our agents here agreed.'

'A personal opinion of the New York police,' said Storm, thinking grimly of O'Halloran, 'is that they're much more negative than positive.' He grinned. 'Of course, I'm not saying that Redhead and Wenlock are the same. But why should he pot us? The little business on deck was enough to annoy, but not enough to call for murder. And' – his face grew hard – 'how did it happen that the crowd on the quay was stampeded by a hold-up at the same time as the shooting? Was it coincidence? Or were the two jobs connected?'

The Assistant Secretary spoke with a rare candour.

'I've been informed of that. To be frank, I wondered.'

Storm proffered cigarettes and lit up.

'Well, Sir William, I'm afraid that's all I can do to help you, although there's one little thing –' He puffed carefully, preparing the coming lie with the necessary gravity of feature. 'I've been having a talk with Grimm, and we've decided that the best thing we can do is to fade away to some unknown spot in the wilds of Scotland, and forget things until the fuss has blown over.'

Sir William beamed.

'I'm very glad to hear it, Mr Storm. We are – er – naturally anxious to – er – handle this matter with the least possible trouble and – er – at no time is it our wish to interfere with the – er – liberties of a citizen.'

'That's exactly what Grimm and I thought,' said Storm affably. 'We'll buzz out of town early tomorrow.'

Sir William shook hands fervently. Seldom, he thought, had he come across a man whose ideas were so admirably suited to his own.

What his thoughts would have been if he had seen the automatics carefully concealed in Storm's pockets was never, fortunately, revealed.

Storm, with the Granvilles well in his mind, spent a brief but interesting period in the Audley Street library, finding a comprehensive directory of Sussex and, to his complete satisfaction, a survey of the history of Ledsholm Grange. The Granville couple, with Letty a good first, interested him largely.

Ledsholm Grange, he gathered, had been in the hands of the Granville family for two hundred years. Once fortified, it possessed, according to the directory, its own chapel, and something approaching fifty rooms. With deepening interest Storm read on:

> The large moat encircling the one-time impregnable fortress and supported by a now crumbling wall is no longer used, although the great drawbridge makes an impressive entry to the drive through the extensive grounds even to this day.
>
> Probably the most striking landmark is the great Black Rock, standing opposite the drawbridge. Carried there by some colossal feat of olden-day engineering, it towers two hundred feet into the air, and its surface is as smooth as satin.

'Ta-rump!' hummed Storm. 'Jolly kind of place, but it must be hellish lonely. Four miles from Ledsholm village, and not a building nearer than three miles! Twenty square miles of private land surrounding it, with only a couple of third class roads running through. Lonely's the word all right.'

A taxi bore him to the flat which he rented in Audley Street – this after a brief shopping expedition and a bite to eat – and he opened the front door with the inward sense of satisfaction which even bachelors experience when returning to the fold. The silence within told him that his manservant, Marcus Horrobin, was still on vacation.

Horrobin was a character. Since entering Storm's service five years before he had often confided that fifteen years as a butler in the house of a Very Great Man made him hate the sight, thought and smell of a title.

'Not, sir, that I would gainsay the claims which any such persons have to quality but one gets, if I may put it so, somewhat *restive*. Moreover to me, a non-smoker, the odour of Lord Mallerby's cigars were overpowering. Since coming into your service, Mr Storm, I can honestly say that in spite of some loss of caste in the eyes of my fellow servitors I –'

'Horrors,' interrupted Storm on the occasion of that particular little outburst, all delivered with incredible fluency and without a change of expression. 'Is my suit laid out?'

'Undoubtedly, sir,' replied Horrors imperturbably. 'Pearl grey socks or maroon?'

'It beats me,' grinned Storm, 'how anybody ever stuck you for fifteen years, you humbug! Maroon.'

In spite of which they managed, in the words of Horrobin, 'to work together admirably and with the least possible wastage of energy'.

The servant had been given a month's leave of absence from the start of the U.S.A. trip and as the 'famous boxers' were home three days before their official time Horrors was excusably missing. Storm grinned as he saw the perfect order of every room; Horrors was a sound fellow.

Then he sniffed and for a moment the grin left his face. Very faintly but very definitely he caught the smell of violet hair oil.

Storm took his automatic from his overcoat pocket. Like a cat he went forward, his ruggedly handsome face set grimly. Without a sound he twisted the handle of the door, flinging it open.

Then he grinned.

It was empty.

'Martin,' he told himself gently, 'you're getting jumpy. There's no-one – tch! Damn you!'

The curse rasped from his lips as something hard struck against his right wrist, sending his gun clattering and a bullet spitting harmlessly into the wall. Feeling angrier than at any time since the attack on Long Island he found himself looking into the cool, mocking eyes of a man whose age, he judged, was on the fifty mark but whose hand, lean and brown, was as steady as a rock round the handle of a threatening automatic.

'You're wrong,' he said quietly, and behind his words was a steely inflexibility. His expression, faintly mocking, was that of a man who holds the whip hand, knows it and is fully capable of using it. 'I've been here for an hour, Storm, waiting for you. And if you'll take the hint, always look behind curtains when searching for intruders.'

Storm managed a grin.

After the first shock of surprise he felt more normal. The very mockery in the other's steely grey eyes forbade panic. With a sudden move he slipped his hand into his pocket, expecting a staccato 'put your hands up!' from the other but without getting it.

'Don't mind if I smoke?' he murmured. 'Splendid. Have one? No? Pity.' Very delicately he sniffed the air. 'Now we know,' he said guilefully, 'where the smell came from. Funny, but I never did like men who used scent.'

The other's smile tightened. He was obviously touchy about the scent accusation, and Storm grinned to himself. From past experience he knew that the surest chink in a man's armour was vanity.

The gunman said stiffly: 'Allow me to congratulate you on a keen sense of smell.'

Storm waved his hand airily.

'Nothing – nothing at all. May I – without impertinence of course – ask you why – ?'

The stranger's mocking grin grew broader. As he pulled a chair nearer, Storm took a full and comprehensive scrutiny. He saw no reason to go back on his earlier estimate of the other's age – the greying hair and the lined face bespoke a man on the wrong side of fifty – but he was impressed by the quiet air of authority. Slight, almost fragile and possessing no remarkable facial characteristic he carried his body well, and from the clean cut of his square chin Storm gathered that he would easily risk the lives or deaths of others, and perhaps his own.

'Well?' murmured Storm encouragingly.

'Well, Mr Storm. To be brief, you have come into contact with an organisation of which I am the English agent.'

'Meaning Redhead?' queried Storm.

'Meaning Redhead,' acknowledged the stranger. He stared hard at Storm and his piercing grey eyes seemed to bore through the other's set expression of cynical amusement. 'I don't know how you came to get in his way, Storm, but it doesn't really matter. Fortunately for you I'm acting off my own bat and am warning you. Redhead is out for blood – your blood. He has an idea that you know more than he wants you to know.'

'Meaning?' queried Storm softly.

The middle-aged gunman pursed his lips, and his words came out slowly but full of meaning.

'He thinks, and I'm not so sure that he's wrong, that you belong to the little organisation called "Z" Department.'

Storm's brows went up.

'What's that? Sounds like a rousing story for the fourth form.'

The other laughed grimly, not wholly satisfied by the response.

'If you don't know, forget it. But – ' He leaned forward a little, intense, impressive. 'Take my advice, and whether you're in "Z" Department or not, get out of the country while the going's good, and take Grimm with you. Otherwise there might be an "accident" –'

He met Storm's cool stare icily. For a second time within the last few days Storm felt that he was gazing into a pair of eyes which could spell death! But with the man on the *Hoveric* he had felt an intense, unreasonable hatred, the hatred of a man of his type for anything and anybody unclean. From the man in the flat the challenge came cleanly. If he crossed swords it would be against someone of his own mettle.

The pregnant silence lasted for a full thirty seconds. Then the stranger curled his lips with the same mocking grin that had illuminated his features throughout the discussion.

'Well?'

Storm stood up, stretching himself idly to his full height.

'With my compliments,' he said easily, 'and with those of Roger Grimm – get out!'

The stranger saw the coming trouble a fraction of a second too late. With the word 'out' Storm shot his great fist downwards, driving with every ounce of strength against the man's biceps. His long reach and the incredible speed with which he moved beat the other, and the automatic, shaken from pain-numbed fingers, clattered to the floor.

But in a trice he was out of his seat, ducking like an eel. For a fierce minute they struggled.

'I think,' panted Storm finally, 'that you'll have to give me best.'

The self-confessed agent of Redhead's organisation went limp in unspoken surrender.

Storm let him go, then swooped on the automatic.

He said lightly: 'You'll hardly believe it, indeed I hardly believe it myself, but I've taken quite a liking to you – on the "our friend the enemy" basis, of course. After all you undoubtedly had a sound chance of potting me in the back a little earlier in the evening and you didn't take it. That suggests that when you said "warning" you meant it.'

The other breathed hard, but the mocking smile still persisted.

'Further,' said Storm mildly, 'I think it was deuced decent of you. Most unlike Redhead – '

He rapped the last words out but there was no change of expression on the other's face. Slowly:

'Not rising to the bait, eh? Well, I want to ask you one or two minor questions and we'll call it square. But keep in mind the bonny boys from that "Z" Department you mentioned. Do you take me?'

'Depends on the questions.'

'You're a cool one,' admitted Storm. 'Well, here goes. Who are you?'

The other seemed to toss a mental coin. In point of fact he was willing enough to vouchsafe information that the authorities already had, although he would have tried to make a break from Storm rather than give away vital stuff. He said at last:

'Since it interests you, I'm known as Zoeman. For some time I operated the English side of the Wenlock Oil Corporation, but twelve months ago I was "retired". Since then,' he added blandly, 'I've been devoting my time to rather less orthodox but more profitable business.'

Storm saw his chance and took it.

'Still on behalf of Wenlock Oils?'

For a moment he saw consternation behind the mask of mockery, but Zoeman recovered himself well.

'What makes you think that?' he asked softly.

Storm grinned genially.

'It is possible I know more than you think. It is unwise to underestimate one's enemy.' It was bluff, but Zoeman's expression showed him it was succeeding. 'However,' Storm added with a cheery grin, 'my row's with Redhead. I don't like him and he doesn't like me – and he's going to hate me a lot more!' He snapped his fingers expressively. 'There you are, Zoeman. Take it or leave it. Purely because you didn't pull the trigger when you could have done I'm going to let you go – but when you get out, stay out!'

Zoeman stood up slowly. He looked at the gun which rested lightly in Storm's hand, and from it his gaze travelled to the lazy blue eyes. The two men stared as they had stared before, the one challenging and the other defiant, but this time Storm held the cards. He had Zoeman guessing and guessing hard, and he had learned that the Wenlock Oil Corporation was well worth looking into.

He knew that Sir William Divot would have been more than perturbed had he known of the situation, but secretly Storm was annoyed at the virtual threat of preventive action by the Government. He had kept the rules by telling the Secretary of the shooting incident, but from the time he had left the Home Office he considered himself a free agent. Nothing the politician had said altered his grim determination to settle with Wenlock. If Wenlock happened to be Redhead – well, it was in the game.

Added to his desire to find Wenlock and a belief that he would do it best by letting Zoeman go, was the unreasonable but nonetheless certain liking that he had formed for the gunman. Possessing a deep if sometimes boisterous sense of humour, the idea that Zoeman was somehow pulling his leg gave a spice to the situation. Divot could go to blazes. Zoeman was going free.

For his part, Zoeman had more than an idea that if Storm did intend to let him go there was some ulterior reason for it lurking at the back of the big man's mind.

He hesitated.

'Oh, blue hades!' exploded Storm. 'There's the door. Use it. I'm going to keep your gun as a small memento. Scoot. Vanish. Run. And do remember me to Ginger!'

6

A Telegram from Granville

Grimm, released from the crowd of relations and friends collected by his parents to greet his triumphant return, looked at Martin Storm as though he was seeing a five-headed dinosaur.

'You really mean,' he breathed, 'that you had him here and you let him go?'

'Certainly I do,' asserted Storm pugnaciously.

'Of all the –'

'Oh, do shut up,' interrupted Storm rudely. 'We haven't time for that, Grimy. He could have plugged me through the back and all you'd have seen of me would have been the coffin. He called it an errand of mercy and I paid him back in the same cloud of righteousness. Kind of armistice.'

'But the war hasn't properly started yet,' said Grimm aggrievedly. 'Oi – what's that?'

'That's more like it,' grinned Storm, revealing the two purchased automatics and that which he had appropriated from Zoeman. 'Now we're armed and ready for anything – I've got silencers, you'll notice. Catch.'

Grimm caught the tossed revolver, worked its mechanism, sniffed, helped himself to a goodly supply of ammunition, and put the lot in his overcoat pocket.

Then he helped himself with the air of a proprietor to Storm's whisky, and lit a cigarette.

'Here's luck, Martin. What's for tomorrow?'

Storm drank and deliberated. Finally:

'First a little inquiry into the Wenlock Oil Corporation. They're in Leadenhall Street according to the telephone book. Then a journey into the country. We'll travel large and all that so that the boys Sir William has almost certainly put on our tail will give the "all clear". Then we can park our stuff and come back when we want to, free citizens of good old England.'

'Where are we going?' demanded Grimm pertinently.

Storm affected to consider.

'Well,' he said slowly, 'somewhere in the country. Now –' He stared at Grimm as though struck suddenly by a brainwave. 'What about the Granvilles and Ledsholm Grange?'

'You darned humbug!' snorted Grimm. 'Trying to make the poor girl's life a misery.'

'Who said anything about a girl?' demanded Storm, slightly red and over-indignant.

'You did,' asserted Grimm. He grinned. 'All right, my lad! Only I won't promise not to try my hand too.'

'As to that, there's not the slightest, wildest chance of.'

Bedecked in a glorious dressing-gown which made even Horrors blink, Storm spent an hour puzzling over the matter of Redhead, Sir William Divot, Zoeman and the Granvilles.

His conclusions, although indefinite enough, gave him a certain measure of satisfaction. Tabulated, they were:

1. Redhead must be classed as a national danger, otherwise the Home Office would not have taken the tone it had.
2. That Sir William was convinced that Storm and Grimm were out of harm's way.
3. That Zoeman was a likeable cuss, but what the devil made him run in harness with a swine like Redhead?
4. That Redhead's belief that he, Storm, knew things about the business, strengthened as it would be by Zoeman's report (if Zoeman ever made one) made it likely that further attacks would materialise, p.d.q.

As it was three o'clock before he slid between the sheets it was not surprising that he slept till ten.

Tea, a shave, a bath, bacon and eggs, a careful selection of socks and tie, accounted for his time up to eleven-thirty. Then he slipped a loaded gun into his pocket and decided to deposit his baggage at Waterloo before going to fetch Grimm.

A sudden thought delayed him. Horrobin would be useful at Ledsholm Grange. He left a note with full instructions for the valet's return.

Picking up his cases he heard a strident whistle in the hall outside the front door of the flat. A second later his knocker reverberated to the thunderous assault of a telegraph boy.

'Mr Martin Storm?'

Storm nodded, and tore open the wire. Then his eyes blazed and his lips tightened.

Come at once Wenlock causing
trouble Granville.

'Any reply, sir?' demanded the boy.

'Give me a form,' said Storm slowly, faced with the need for quick decision and uncertain what to do.

The doubt did not concern his response to the wire for the telegraph boy greased off, richer by an undeserved half-crown and an injunction from Storm to get his reply – '*Coming next train Storm*' – off quicker than any wire in the history of the Post Office. But he was uncertain whether to inform Sir William Divot that Wenlock was in the Ledsholm vicinity.

Storm imagined that the gangster – if Wenlock was Redhead – had fallen for the girl, so that she was in danger up to a point in any case. But he fancied that if the police started poking about in the Ledsholm neighbourhood Wenlock might think the girl or her brother had caused the trouble; and the danger to Letty would be colossal. No. The Assistant Secretary would get the news at a later date.

He discovered that a train, calling at Ledsholm Halt, left Waterloo at twelve-fifty-five. He hurtled into a taxi and told the driver to move quicker than blazes.

In exactly nine minutes he was entering the hall of the Philmore Crescent house. In one minute before the train was due to depart he dragged his cousin into the station with a sigh of relief.

Safe at last in their compartment he poked the telegram in front of Grimm's generous nose. Realising that the personal element was developing fast, Grimm made little comment, even to the point of agreeing – or more accurately, not disagreeing – when Storm passed on his decision to keep Sir William uninformed.

Reaching Ledsholm Halt it proved to be a cockeyed station serving the small village through which it ran and the scattered farms and hamlets within a five mile area. Although they had left London in brilliant sunshine, rain was now streaming down, beating the rough surface of the road with all the fury of a hail storm.

'Wonder if there'll be anyone to meet us,' murmured Storm as he handed the tickets to a surly-looking guard.

Outside they saw a bedraggled horse and cab, but there was no sign of a driver.

A weather-beaten, wind-swaying signboard opposite declared to the world at large that the drably painted inn before which it hung rejoiced in the name of *The Four Bells* A smaller notice bore the name *Benjamin Cripps*.

There was no-one in sight, only the length of a winding street lashed by rain.

'Lord,' groaned Storm, taking a firm grip of his two cases and cursing the weather, the village, and the cabby. 'Better try the pub, hadn't we?'

They dashed across the puddled road and burst into the bar parlour of *The Four Bells,* deposited their dripping bags and looked round with interest.

To their surprise the effect was pleasing. Everything about the inside of Benjamin Cripps' hostelry was as bright and glistening as everything outside was drab. Even the five occupants of the parlour fell under the spell of its cheer.

Leaving their bags by the door they crossed to the bar, behind which a short, podgy little man was polishing glasses with comfortable energy.

'Good afternoon, gentlemen. What can I have the pleasure?'

'Two whiskies,' said Storm pleasantly. Knowing better than to try and hurry natives of the Sussex Downs he waited with patience until the drinks arrived, taking meanwhile a brief look at the other occupants of the cosy parlour.

The station guard was leaning lazily against the bar, while a ragged-coated rustic, obviously the cabby, stared vacantly through the window. The two others were commercials from the look of them, waiting for the next train to town. But they were toughish-looking commercials. As he looked away he caught the furtive gleam of their lowered eyes which were officially regarding the brown ale reposing temporarily in their tankards.

Storm smiled at the innkeeper and raised his glass.

'Here's luck,' he toasted. 'Drinks all round, on me.'

Mine host beamed and set to work. The cabby jerked into instant life, while the station guard murmured a polite thanks. The commercials merely grunted.

'Nasty day,' commented Benjamin Cripps when his task was done. 'Travelling far, sirs?'

'I don't know,' admitted Storm, who had been waiting for the question. 'I'm going to Ledsholm Grange, but there doesn't seem to be much in the way of a cab about.'

Benjamin Cripps beamed on them.

'Well I never! Then ye'll be the quality young Mr Granville was talking about!'

Storm grinned affably.

'He was expecting me,' he admitted. 'Has he been down?'

Mr Cripps shook his head.

'Not since yester night, sir, but he telephoned a while ago. "Ben," says he – having known me since he were so high – "if two gentlemen should happen to be on the next train, see that they're made comfortable like and that I'll be meeting them by three o'clock".' Ben looked brightly at the grandfather clock in a corner. 'Which means he won't be more'n another ten minutes, he being a punctual gentleman if ever there was one.'

'Good,' smiled Storm, and felt Grimm's arm nudge his.

Out of the corner of his eye he saw one of the commercials walking quickly towards the street door. Mr Cripps' rubicund face gaped in astonishment.

'Well, I never did! Fancy going out into rain like that, and the next train not due for an hour!'

Storm looked across at the second commercial, feeling the man's furtive scrutiny, noticing his swarthy face and powerful body.

He might be wrong, but it was all Europe to a suburban back garden that the men were not at the inn by sheer coincidence. It was only too easy to imagine them as emissaries of Redhead, and the probability made Storm go chill.

Then he thought of the slim, adorable figure of Letty Granville, reminding him that Redhead, as Wenlock, was butting in on a matter which engaged his, Storm's, personal attentions very seriously.

His lips pressed together in a firm line. Grimm saw the signs and a ghost of a grin played about his rugged face.

'Wonder who they are,' he murmured, taking advantage of mine host's preoccupation.

'We'll keep an eye open,' said Storm briefly.

The words were hardly out of his mouth when the sound of a heavy car speeding along the wet road came to their ears. It stopped outside *The Four Bells.*

A moment later the door swung open and Granville stepped inside. Looking towards him with a welcoming smile, Storm felt suddenly that he was seeing a ghost.

Granville's face was almost devoid of colour. Lines were engraved there which the cousins had not seen before. But his smile was genuine as he gripped their hands with a hard, nervous clasp.

'Lord! It's decent of you to come. I don't know what – '

'It'll wait,' snapped Storm, with an eye on the remaining commercial and a thought for the cocked ears of Mr Cripps. 'Let's get away from here before you talk.'

He lifted his cases and pushed through the door, with Grimm after him and Granville bringing up the rear. As he moved towards the car he glimpsed through the windows of the village post office the broad back of the commercial who had just left Benjamin Cripp's comfortable parlour; the man was speaking into a telephone.

The door of the shop had been carelessly left open and Storm moved quickly towards it. The man's voice, thick with anger, pierced the walls of the booth and came faintly to the listener's ears.

'Say! Are you dames sappy? What about my number? Yep, number! Heck! Mayfair one-eight-double-ought-three!'

Storm could have hugged himself. Not only was he given freely the fact that the fellow was an American, but presented in addition with what could be a vital telephone number.

Still keeping in the shadow of the door he heard the American give sudden vent to a stream of lurid Bowery profanity, glimpsed the shocked face of the village postmistress.

Storm was fully aware of the irritation which the telephone service could create, but he disliked the Bowery tough's outburst nearly as much as he disliked the thought that he was one of Redhead's spies. His voice rapped out like the lash of a whip.

'Cut that out!'

The American spun round like a miniature tornado and almost before Storm realised it his hand was inside his pocket. Storm covered three yards of floor space in a split second, crashing his fist into the man's face. Grunting, the other staggered back, the force of the blow dragging his hand down from the butt of a wicked-looking gun.

Storm's long fingers whipped up the gun in a flash. He looked mockingly at the American.

'There's a difference,' he said coldly, 'between England and the U.S.A. Also, if I know anything about the bright lad who runs you, you're in for a nasty time when he learns that you shouted his telephone number about the village.'

The man's brutal face was distorted in rage; Storm knew that the telephone gibe had struck home. But for the time being he had to manoeuvre the two 'commercials' away without creating too much of a sensation. Luckily the still teeming rain kept most of the villagers out of the streets.

'Now,' he ordered, 'keep well back in here but keep in sight of the door while I'm outside. And if you think of dodging remember that I am just that much quicker with a gun than you. Now move!'

The gunman glowered, but the odds were too heavy. He watched Storm reach the door and heard his deep, pleasant voice as he spoke quietly to the startled postmistress.

'I'm very much afraid,' said Storm gently, realising that the woman's nerves were dangerously near breaking-point, 'that we've come across a bandit. But there's no need to worry. I'll fetch one or two of my friends and we'll handle him. For the time being it would be much wiser to talk as little as possible about this.'

With luck the postmistress would take him for a detective and fall in with what he said. Stepping briskly towards the door but being careful to keep his man covered without showing the gun to anyone outside, he peered towards the car.

'Now, son. Move again and move quickly. When you see your pal on the other side of the road call him over but don't try any tricks.'

The gunman began to move, while Storm kept well out of his reach to make sure there was no sudden, desperate attempt to wrest the automatic from him.

Grimm, seeing what was happening, slipped into the road, his hand thrust well down into his trousers pocket, clasping his unseen automatic. At the same moment the gunman raised his nasal voice.

'Say! Lefty!'

Lefty, in the doorway of *The Four Bells,* gave a sudden start.

Storm watched him strolling sluggishly across the road, and wished that the man would take his hand out of his pocket.

The thought was hardly out of his head when the man in front of him ducked suddenly, raising his thick voice in a wild warning which rang like a clarion call through the deserted, rain-swept street.

'Plug him, Lefty!'

Like greased lightning Lefty's hand ripped from his pocket and Storm saw a jab of yellow flame spit from a revolver. No sound came but the *zutt* of a silenced gun, but the shot, murderously quick though it was, came a shade too late.

Storm dropped a fraction of a second before the bullet hummed. He heard the crack of breaking glass and as he took quick aim and fired point black at Lefty he hoped to heaven that the postmistress was out of harm's way.

The silence of the street was ripped again as Lefty, dropping his automatic, mouthed a stream of searing curses.

Blood was streaming from his arm, showing that Storm's shot had taken him just above the right wrist. Before the first gunman could jerk upwards Grimm had whipped round the Daimler, gun in hand.

A grim smile played round the corners of Storm's mouth as he heard windows jerking upwards and saw the door of *The Four Bells* open. He spoke quietly to Grimm.

'Get 'em in the back of the car, Roger, and don't let the cusses budge. Granny – ' Granville was already out of the car, staring in bewilderment. 'You'd better come with me. We've got to kid these folk,' Storm went on, 'that we – Grimm and I – are detectives who came down to look after Ledsholm Grange. Rig up a cock-and-bull story of a threat of murder or robbery. That should let us get clear. Savvy?'

Granville savvied with admirable presence of mind. Within ten minutes the inhabitants of Ledsholm village were agog with the story of bandits who had opened fire on the Post Office prior to carrying out a raid on the Grange. The story, eminently reasonable in view of the reports of outrages which filled the daily Press, was swallowed as quickly as Benjamin Cripps' brown ale.

Storm finished with a brief, soothing and complimentary word to the still trembling postmistress, then crowded into the back of the Daimler, with the gunmen for company.

They were huddled up in a corner with their hands in front of them, and Storm realised that they were two of the toughest specimens that he had ever set eyes on. He shivered at the thought of gentry of their kind keeping a watch on Letty Granville.

Showing them the gleaming steel of his gun, he commented affably: 'They call this "going for a ride", don't they?'

The smouldering hate in the furtive eyes of the gunmen changed to fear. They jerked forward.

'Say, Boss!'

'Get back!' snapped Storm. 'That's better. Now, if it eases your rotten minds, your country's connotation of that phrase will not be carried out – just yet. But' – he glared at them – 'it's ten chances to one on your fading out of this little planet, and fading very soon! Think it over. Maybe it'll help you to talk later on. But there's just one thing now. Where's Redhead?'

He learned all he wanted to know from their faces. They were Redhead's men without a shadow of doubt, and they were tough. Not a word came from their lips in spite of their fear.

'Rest easy,' grinned Storm.

It was anything but a comfortable ride, yet as the powerful Daimler swung into the drive of Ledsholm Grange he hardly realised that they were at their destination. He was satisfied with the day's work so far. The first score was to him, for the thugs in the back of the car were admirable hostages.

Driving the two gangsters in front of him he followed Grimm and Granville up a short flight of steps leading to the main hall. Inside, he grinned cheerfully at Granville.

Then he remembered the telegram and the fact that he had no idea why the younger man had sent for him.

Something in Granville's eyes sent a shiver of fear through him. His voice was low and strained.

'Now – what's the trouble?'

But it was Grimm, who had been able to talk during the journey, who answered.

'Prepare for a nasty jolt, old boy. Wenlock, curse him, has got hold of Letty!'

7

A MATTER OF NUMBERS

The two thugs were bound hand and foot and tied to a bed in one of the many rooms in the great building. A gardener – Perriman – one of four servants at the Grange who had prepared a royal welcome for the wanderers' return and were murderously inclined towards the devils who had abducted Miss Letty, were keeping watch outside the locked door and hopefully clutching a poker.

Storm, Granville and Grimm made a cheerless trio in the great reception hall.

'The first thing we saw when we reached here,' said Granville wearily, 'was Wenlock's ruddy ginger thatch! You could have sent me flying with a matchstick! I didn't dream –'

He broke off, passing a hand through his hair, then went on quickly, as though anxious to get the story over.

'Of course Harries – the caretaker – didn't know that he wasn't the friend he had made himself out to be when he had called half-an-hour before our arrival last night.

'Anyhow, Wenlock was civil enough if you discount his outrageous suggestion that we should let the Grange to him for six months, with an option for another six. He said that we might as well stay for another year as we've been away so long.

'Letty wouldn't speak to him at all, while I told him pretty bluntly that we neither cared for him, or wanted to hear from him from now until doomsday. He went away quietly enough, and we'd hoped that we'd never come across the blighter again.

'Harries, his wife and the two gardeners, who put themselves out to make a show for us, did their best to calm things down a bit, but the homecoming was a frost. I wished I'd pressed you two fellows to come straight down here with us, and Letty agreed – '

'Did she say so?' interposed Storm off-handedly.

Granville nodded.

'She said so first, actually. Anyhow, after she'd gone to bed Harries told me that he thought he saw a circle of light in the grounds. Sure enough, there were at least half-a-dozen lights, coming, I reckoned, from torches!

'It didn't take much thinking about. Wenlock was out for trouble. Harries rummaged round and found a couple of blunderbusses, and the other servants posted themselves near Letty's room.

'It was pretty ghoulish, I can tell you! This place, which hasn't been occupied apart for three or four downstairs rooms for nearly five years, was like a beastly sepulchre! We heard things that weren't and saw things that never have been! Talk about ghosts!

'Of course, we didn't worry Letty. But after an hour of it, with the lights still moving about in the grounds, I called up Lewes Police Station.

'I thought we'd be all right then. Someone promised to send half-a-dozen men along to investigate, and about half-an-hour afterwards a car arrived with six or seven men in it. One was in uniform and the rest were in ordinary civvies. Of course I didn't dream –

'It was all over in a flash! The first thing I saw when I opened the door was a nasty-looking gun pushed towards my middle and three others pointed at Harries and the gardeners. I did try to kick the door shut' – Granville smiled wanly – 'but Wenlock socked me with the butt of a gun.

'That was the end of it for me. I woke up an hour or two afterwards, to find Harries and the others tied up like a lot of sacks, and Letty gone!'

Granville stopped for a moment. The bond between himself and his sister, strengthened by five years' travelling together, was a strong one, and the disaster which had overtaken her bit deep. He stood up suddenly, driving one clenched fist into the other open palm.

Overwrought, thought Storm. But he wished Granville didn't gesture quite so theatrically. Still...

'Don't let it get you down,' he encouraged. 'We'll fix it.'

Well, I was all for going straight to the police,' Granville went on. 'It was obvious that the telephone wires had been tampered with, of course – but we found a note stuck to the inside of the front door. After reading it I just felt that I couldn't move. Then it struck me that you two were useful johnnies so I sent one of the gardeners into the village to send the wire and to get a local plumber fellow to see what he could do with the telephone wires.'

Granville took an envelope from his pocket and handed it over. The letter inside was typewritten and unsigned, but Storm could easily understand why it had distressed Granville. He held the letter so that Grimm could read it. They leaned forward beneath the light of the hanging chandelier which spread its glow over the massive dignity of the hall and its sober furnishings. The silence was oppressive and somehow threatening.

My dear Granville,

I have no doubt you are feeling angry. Take my very sound advice before you decide to do something foolish.

Your sister's life depends entirely on your behaviour. You must leave Ledsholm Grange immediately, with the servants, and give me a written leave of tenancy for six months, with an option for another six. You will not come near the Grange during that period.

You will not communicate with the police or any similar body. Not only would it be useless, but your charming sister would lose her life – painfully.

You will signify your acceptance of these terms and your wish to see me again by showing a green light in the front porch of the Grange from ten o'clock until ten-thirty tomorrow, Friday, evening.

Storm seemed to see the redheaded man's eyes with their basilisk expression of malevolent, soulless hatred staring up from the white paper. Involuntarily he shuddered, and when he looked up he saw Grimm's face filled with that same unreasoning, chilled expression of dread.

The sinister influence of the writer of the letter bit through the atmosphere of the lofty hall into their very bones. Granville stared at them tensely.

At last Storm heaved himself upwards from his chair and his deep voice boomed out, calm and confident.

'So-ho, Redhead! It's between us, is it? Well – have a care, my hearty!'

Grimm grinned. Granville's expression eased.

Storm thwacked him heavily on the back.

'That's more like it! Now then. We know a thing or two. Redhead wants Ledsholm Grange and wants it badly. We don't know why, but we can find out. Meanwhile Letty's as safe as houses. Why? Because he's holding her as a kind of barter for the Grange, and if he loses her' – Storm passed gently over the possibility of Redhead's murderous rage getting the better of him – 'he knows he's as much chance of getting the Grange as a cat has of rearing carthorses. Our game is to stall. Keep putting him off, and maybe we'll get a chance of sending him to join the two boys upstairs.'

He beamed round, noting with satisfaction that the strained expression in Granville's eyes was lessening. Nevertheless Granville had had a nasty shock.

'The reasoning's all right,' admitted Grimm after a pause. 'The thing is –'

'The waiting!' burst out Granville, jumping from his chair and pacing the hall nervously. 'Damn it, Storm, we've got to do something! Don't you see? While Letty's with that – swine! – anything might happen. Can't you see?'

Again Storm had a half-reluctant wish that Granville wouldn't make his outbursts quite so melodramatic. But he placed a steadying hand on the younger man's shoulder and looked squarely into his brown eyes.

'I can see, Granville. It's biting me as hard as it is you. But talking won't help – not that kind of talking anyhow. It'll just cloud your judgement and land us in more trouble. What you've got to do is to think, and think like hell, for any reason he might have for wanting the Grange.'

Granville managed a not very heroic grin.

'Where'd you keep your whisky?' demanded Martin. 'There it is, Grimy. Cart it over.'

Grimm brought the decanter and glasses, and after a brief interval for refreshment the cousins – after Granville had been despatched to Harries with an inquiry as to any local activities which might throw some light on Redhead's mysterious anxiety to get possession of the Grange – discussed those odd points of the affair which stuck out so inconsistently.

One thing seemed moderately certain and could explain a great deal.

Redhead's journey to England had been made to fit in with the return of the Granvilles. He had endeavoured to get into the good books of the couple during the trip, failing dismally with Frank, though scoring well enough with Letty. The arrival of Storm had smashed through his plans. Undoubtedly Redhead, as Wenlock, had good reason to hate the cousins.

And now, careering like a couple of rogue-elephants, they had burst into the middle of the shindy at the Grange, picked up a couple of Redhead's pet thugs and written 'setback' on his local progress. His knife would be waiting for Storm and Grimm, and it was a knife likely to carry poison on its blade.

Together with the obvious numerical strength of the enemy and Redhead's cunning, this point engaged the minds of the cousins. Finally:

'Roughly speaking,' said Storm, 'and assuming that we're not going to make an immediate report to Whitehall, we ought to have at least half-a-dozen men.'

'Be better to tell Divot, wouldn't it?' demurred Grimm.

Storm nursed his pipe.

'I know you don't mean that, Roger, or I'd throw you out of the window. Listen. If we bring the police down here, Redhead will realise that there isn't a half chance of his ever gaining possession of the place. And we've got to consider the personal element – '

'The girl,' admitted Grimm.

'And,' said Storm without heeding the interruption, 'we can be sure that if Redhead sees he's beaten off the Grange, she won't stand half a chance. Even you ought to be able to see that. We can hold the blighter off a bit, but we daren't do anything with the police – yet.'

Grimm nodded slowly.

'I see up to a point, Martin. But surely *you* see that the job's too much for us as we are? We want – '

'Reinforcements,' put in Storm. 'That's just what I was saying. Think hard, Roger. Then guess.'

For twenty seconds there was no sound in the room but the rhythmic puffing peculiar to pipe smokers. Then;

'The Arran Twins,' suggested Grimm quietly.

'The Arran Twins!' agreed Storm with a sigh of content. 'And their bodyguard. Hand me that telephone – quick, darn you!'

At a time when Martin Storm and Roger Grimm had been out of England on one of their periodical explorations, exciting things had happened in England.*

The Twins had been active participants, and not only they, but several eager and energetic young men with money, brains and a carefully disguised patriotism.

Storm had no doubt at all that the Twins would not only come but that they would jump to it. But as he lifted the receiver and gave the Mayfair number of the Arrans' flat it struck him forcefully that the line might be tapped. His conversation with the Twins would have to be garbled.

At the other end of the wire a staid but resigned valet – 'Splits' to the Twins' intimates – walked warily towards a bathroom from which came loud sounds of exuberant splashing.

After two minutes Storm heard a plaintive voice drawling over the wire.

'Oh, I say! Who the – blinkin' – hell is – that? Darn it, you might have picked a better moment!'

'Rabbits!' snorted Storm. 'Listen, Timothy' – the Twins were always easily distinguishable, Timothy being long-winded and Tobias talking with machine-gun precision – 'It's Storm here – yes, darn you! Windy. Do you happen to know Ledsholm? Yes, the place in Sussex. You're not coming down this way, are you? No? Only I'm likely to be here for a day or two and I thought – Oh, shut up, curse you, and let me get a word in! Listening? Hump. Well, you remember that little do you went to with Chubby Spencer?'

Until that moment a series of snorts, indicating strong indignation, had travelled over the wire. They stopped suddenly.

'Well,' Storm went on, 'I've found another man who wants the same kind of job done for him. Oh Lord no, there's no real hurry. Anytime within the next hour or two'll do. Yes, round in Bond Street, Timothy. I can't manage it myself. Eh? Oh, I'm getting on so-so, old son. Raining like hell here, though, and I can't get out. Be glad when I get back to town and see some friendly faces. Who? Well, Best and Thrale are holding that little show, aren't they? I don't know who else is going. Milhowel and Dane, eh? Quite enough too, if I know anything about them. Get plenty of beer. Oh – oi, Timothy!' His voice rose urgently, for the especial benefit of anyone who might be listening in. 'Oi – I thought you'd gone, old son. Listen, I've just remembered what I wanted to ring you about. I've a date at the *Carilon*– Fluffy Vere – tell her I'm sorry will you, and I can't possibly get away. Yes, take her yourself if you want to. I don't mind. All right, Tim, thanks. See you some time.'

Timothy Arran, a different man from the one he had been five minutes before, left the telephone and swung round to the waiting Splits.

'Splits, take that blankety telephone and get Toby to come back, quickly. He's at the Junior Conservative. Tell him to round up Derek Milhowel, Martin Best, St John Dane and Dodo Trale. They're to bring enough things for a couple of nights, anyhow. Then ring the garage and tell Sparks I want the Bentley and the Bugatti, ready for long travel at once.'

Meanwhile at Ledsholm Grange, Martin Storm was assuring Frank Granville that trouble, and large trouble, was on the way for Ginger Wenlock.

'One day,' rasped Granville, 'I'll get my hands on that devil, and – '

He stopped, swinging round like lightning. Storm's hand was at his side but he didn't touch his gun. Grimm, with his back to the door, sat dead still, frozen.

'What will you do?' demanded a voice, suave and charged with a sinister, threatening power.

Like men in a dream they saw Wenlock, a squat, gleaming revolver in his right hand.

* *Men, Maids, and Murder* by John Creasey. Melrose.

8

TROUBLE AT THE GRANGE

'And how the devil,' asked Storm, 'did you get here?'

'Walked in,' said Wenlock, but there was no humour in his green eyes. 'You imagined that an addle-headed countryman would be good enough to warn you, didn't you, Storm? Well – as with other things you must change your mind. And quickly!'

'Hm-hm,' murmured Storm, thinking desperately. 'Talk on, pretty man, talk on.'

Wenlock glowered.

'You trumpety fool! I'm tired of you! You're getting a nuisance, Storm. I – '

'No threats,' pleaded Storm blandly, wagging an admonitory finger. 'Listen, Big Boy. You're scared stiff to do anything which might harm Grimm or myself because you know the interest of the Men Who Matter hovers over us. And remember I left information as to where I was going when I left London.'

Wenlock hesitated. Storm's quick-tongued attack had been shrewder than he knew. Wenlock's own doubts and fears that if anything happened to the cousins the plans which he had carefully laid and which were set for a colossal reward would be destroyed, returned to him. A false step now would mean ruin – ruin when he was tantalisingly near success.

His green eyes gazed with devilish intensity at Storm.

'One day, you interfering bastard, I'll kill you!'

'Language, language,' chided Storm automatically. He was fairly confident that there was no immediate danger. If Wenlock's object had been simply to kill them he had little doubt that he would have done so. What was lurking in that tortuous brain?

The man was now leaning back against a massive table. At the main door of the great hall three tough specimens, as hard-bitten as the two upstairs, lolled lazily, badly rolled cigarettes dangling from their lips. Each man carried a gun and showed it.

Gangster rule in England! Ten days before, Storm would have scoffed at the thought. But it was here. The men in front of him were killers.

'I intend,' said Wenlock bitingly, 'to take complete possession of this house. Whether I have to kill you in order to do so doesn't matter. I'm going to get it.'

'A challenge to the gods indeed,' murmured Storm.

'I have every reason,' went on Wenlock, speaking with carefully chosen words which did nothing to rob his eyes of their glowing malevolence, 'to believe that you have just "disappeared into the country". Thus it would not be remarkable if you failed to return for a while. At the same time I want to make sure that I am not discovered in this neighbourhood, and it is just possible that your protracted absence might lead to inquiries. Therefore I would – '

'Rather have a peaceful evacuation,' interpolated Storm. 'What's your bait, little man? How do you propose to hook us?'

Wenlock's green eyes shimmered malignantly.

'Shall we say – the girl?'

Careful watcher though he was he failed to see the hardening of Storm's mouth and the slightly more aggressive sweep of his jaw.

'If you get out,' said Wenlock, 'and persuade Granville to get out, I will return Miss Granville – unharmed. If you don't' – he paused for effect, and got it – 'I will deliver her – dead!'

Only the pressure of Storm's arm on Granville's elbow kept the younger man from throwing himself at the tall, red-haired devil who stared with those horrible green eyes.

Storm tugged at his underlip.

'In England,' he began mildly, 'murder is – '

'One more or less makes no difference to me,' replied Wenlock. 'I'll give you an hour to decide. Take it or leave it. If you leave it you'll be as cold as the girl, and you'll never get word through to London. The telephone wires have been cut again, both cars in the garage are useless, and there are twenty men in the grounds to stop you from getting away.'

He swung round, snapping instructions to one of the men at the door, who went swiftly towards the passage leading to the staircase. They reappeared quickly, with the two prisoners taken in Ledsholm village. Without another word Wenlock went out, taking the two erstwhile prisoners with him. Only the men at the door remained, their guns very much in evidence.

The air seemed cleaner when he had gone, but the full meaning of his words struck home with a chilling impact.

At considerable risk and with a large portion of luck they might overcome the three swarthy gunmen on the threshold, but they knew that Wenlock had not exaggerated his forces much. Even a dozen men in the grounds would turn a sortie into suicide.

Storm glanced at the clock standing in the corner of the hall. Its hands pointed to half-past four, which meant that the talk with Timothy Arran had been finished less than fifty minutes. But Wenlock's reference to the telephone wires made it certain that he knew nothing of the summons for help.

Was there a chance of rescue?

He turned his back on the three gunmen but was careful not to touch his pockets.

Granville stared at him, white-faced.

'This means we're beaten, Storm.'

'What-ho!' beamed Storm, not without effort. 'If the worst comes to the worst we'll have to let 'em have it.'

With Letty Granville in Wenlock's hands they were, indeed, helpless. The devil of it was that if they surrendered the Grange and went to the police, Wenlock would get back at them. Of course, it looked easy enough to double-cross Wenlock, but –

The Home Office would not have worried itself half dead over the man had he not been a menace. Wenlock, police or no police, was a living danger. They were up against a brick wall.

And the only alternative to an unpleasant death was unconditional surrender!

He sought desperately in his mind for a means of gaining time until the Twins arrived. The minutes flew and Wenlock's hour was nearly up.

Suddenly he laughed, a harsh and mirthless sound, making Grimm look at him sharply, and sending Granville's head up with a jerk.

'Bright boys, aren't we? After all, we're not dead yet. If we clear out we shall get Letty back and all we've got to do is to take a nice long holiday.'

He beamed happily on the grim-visaged, sullen-eyed gangsters. That they were products of America's crime wave was certain. But where did they hide? What part of the surrounding country sheltered them? How did Wenlock manage to muster them at the Grange, even allowing for the loneliness of the great building, without rumours getting round which demanded investigation?

He gave it up as his plan matured slowly. Grimm broke the short silence.

'How'd you know Wenlock will do as he says?'

Storm, his back towards the three gunmen, winked meaningly, careful to keep his hands in view. He knew that if the gangsters lost sight of one hand for a split second they would shoot.

'We'd have to trust him. I believe he'd come across.'

From the corner of his eye he saw one of the gunmen heave his thickset body from the door post and lurch towards the others. There followed a brief dialogue spoken so low that Storm failed to catch a word before the man who had moved tucked his gun in his pocket and went bullishly down the short flight of steps leading from the hall door.

Storm was satisfied. The gangster had swallowed his bait and it was ten pounds to an orange pip that he was taking the news of the 'surrender' talk to Wenlock. With Ginger lulled into a sense of security a desperate sortie such as Storm was crazily planning had a better chance of success. But the chance was perilously thin.

If he had believed in Wenlock's good faith he might have made the peaceful evacuation; there were few things that he wouldn't have done for Letty Granville. But he had a pretty shrewd idea that were they to get a hundred yards away from the Grange they would find themselves ambushed.

Storm had a hunch that the only reason for Wenlock's hour of inactivity was that the red-haired man was desperately anxious to make sure there was no disturbance at the Grange which could reach outside ears. The cold-bloodedness which was an integral part of the man's make-up was being held in check only by reasons of exigency.

Glancing meaningfully at Grimm and Granville, he played with the buttons of his waistcoat, revealing first three and then two; dumb-play was safer than whispering.

Grimm raised his brows a fraction. Granville frowned.

Tantalisingly Storm wandered about the corner of the hall. His back to the men, he flicked his eyes towards a heavy sofa. His meaning was clear.

If we can get behind the sofa, my hearties, we'll have some kind of cover. Shall we take a chance?

His question was answered by a barely-concealed eagerness in Granville's eyes and a barely-perceptible nod from Grimm.

Storm stretched his great body upwards, arms wide apart and high above his head in a gargantuan yawn. Taking two long strides forward and bringing a sudden wariness to the eyes of the gunmen he grinned engagingly, bringing his hands to rest lightly on the back of a solid oak occasional chair.

It happened in a flash. Gripping the chair he heaved it upwards before crashing it towards the gangsters. They ducked simultaneously and the chair winged over their heads, crashing against the wall but catching them as it rebounded.

In a flash Storm dived backwards and as the first shot spat out he dropped behind the cover. Frank Granville was already there while Grimm, behind a great armchair dragged next to the couch, was equally safe.

The gangsters mouthed a stream of oaths as the bullets from their guns bit into the stout leather, but the thick upholstery closed round the messengers of death, taking away their bite. The faces of both Americans were distorted with fury as they fired, cursing and bellowing.

Beneath the storm of profanity Storm muttered:

'Can you get a grip on the bottom, Granville? Good. Roger, slide your chair over to the sideboard. We'll follow.'

Before the gangsters saw the ruse, it had succeeded. The sofa seemed to slide along the polished floor and as the great armchair joined it formed a barricade round one end of the enormous oak sideboard, fitting snugly to the wall opposite the door. With almost superhuman strength Storm and Grimm, getting small purchase with their fingers on the edge of the sideboard, slewed it round until one end was at an angle of thirty-five degrees from the wall. With the settee and chair it made a small but effective pill-box, secure against the revolver fire of Wenlock's thugs, secure even against rifle-shooting.

Storm squinted across to the grandfather clock still ticking away the seconds. It was nearly half-past five, but their new position gave them breathing space. The message to the twins was now nearly two hours old; if they came by car they might arrive at any time.

Before the sudden manoeuvre Storm had worked the position out and taken what seemed to be the most likely chance.

First, if Letty was anywhere near the Grange, when Wenlock learned of the development it might prove fatal. But he played on a hunch that she had been taken out of the neighbourhood, and he prayed that his hunch was right.

Second, he had deliberated whether to pack themselves in or whether to make a dive for freedom. The latter was almost impossible, for Wenlock's numerical strength was high. On top of which, if the twins and their bodyguard arrived they would be running into the arms of Wenlock without anything to fight for. Staying in the hall but keeping Wenlock at bay was obviously the only course to take.

He had little fears about the twins running blindly into trouble. The telephone message carried a warning and an exhortation to bring guns, and bring them quickly; and he knew his men.

Crouching back against the wall they could see nothing of the two gunmen who had apparently realised that they were out-manoeuvred, for no matter from what angle the barricade was approached it afforded safe cover. Storm heard a chamber being reloaded and an oath-strewn muttering. A moment later one of the gunmen moved towards the staircase.

The chance was devilishly tempting. With only one man in front they had a sound chance of reaching him before reinforcements arrived.

But there was twenty feet of space to cross, and in that twenty feet one automatic could speak a dozen times.

'Doggo's the game,' signalled Storm.

Across the near silence of the great hall came the sudden sharp staccato sound of footsteps.

The red-haired devil's voice came to them, trembling with repressed fury.

'I'll give you two minutes to come out!' he rasped.

Storm managed a chuckle.

'You really expect us to do that?'

He could almost see the beetroot red suffusing Wenlock's sandy skin as a curse spat out.

'Let them have it, Pedro!'

The words made Storm wonder. Let them have what?

The answer came with a shivering suddenness which made even Storm's face blanch. Across the momentary silence blasted the spitting tap-tap-tap of machine-gun fire!

Bullet after bullet bit into the sofa, tearing remorselessly through the upholstery and padding. Before the staring eyes of the three trapped men the back of the couch bulged outwards. Like living ghosts, hot-eyed and haggard with the damning of their hopes, they saw the first jagged tear in the leather. Then came another – and another –

Granville cursed as the first rasping bullet came through the hole, striking into the oak panels of the wall and sending splinters flying backwards. A second hummed a few inches from Grimm's nose. A third cracked against the sideboard.

Pressed back as far as they could from the ominous split in the leather all three stared at the stream of bullets coming with devilish speed through the hole. Storm felt an awful hopelessness, a dull, bitter rage. Grimm seemed paralysed. Granville, under fire for the first time in his life, clenched his fingers and bit into his lips to stop himself from breaking down.

The machine-gun rattled on. Its deadly tap-tap-tap came with fear-inspiring regularity. Remorselessly the frayed hole in the leather widened. Bullets streamed two inches from their faces.

'I can't stand it!' groaned Granville. 'I can't – '

Storm gripped his arm. The horror of that creeping death! God!

Then the gun stopped.

They heard Wenlock's voice, thick with rage; Pedro's answer, surly and gruff.

'Cawn't help it, Bawse. Jammed. Mebbe I soon fix it.'

Wenlock spoke again, his voice harsh and remorseless. Storm knew that nothing would stop the murderous attack, nothing would stop the killing.

'Damn you bohunks! Use your guns!'

Almost on his words an automatic spat out, sending a bullet through the hole and thudding against the wall. A second – a third –

Then Pedro's sluggish voice:

'I done it, Bawse.'

Storm groaned. Grimm felt sick. Once that spitting stream started again it spelt the end!

It came; murderously, devilishly. Granville moaned.

'Oh, God!'

Tap-tap-tap! Tap-tap-tap! Tap-tap-tap!

'Oh, God!' burst out Granville, 'I can't stand it!'

Storm gripped his arm, controlling himself with a tremendous effort. They were all white-faced, unnerved by the horror, looking death in the face.

Tap-tap-tap! Tap-tap-tap! Tap-tap-tap!

Each bullet crept closer.

Then for the first time the sound of a shot fired without a silencer broke across the hum. The deadly tapping stopped and Pedro's thick voice wavered upwards in bewilderment.

'Gawd – Bawse! I'm – shot – up!'

Wenlock's furious cursing streamed out, but across it came a sharp, steely voice.

To Grimm the voice was unknown. To Storm it was familiar; soft, steely, mocking.

'Keep looking ahead, Wenlock. And the rest of you. I'm a dozen strong – and I don't mind shooting fellows like you in the back!'

It was Zoeman!

Zoeman, the 'English agent' who had given Storm his warning on the previous night!

9

ENTER THE TWINS

Never a particularly pious young man, Martin Storm's belief in miracles had been negligible until that moment. But thereafter it became a deep and profound faith. Nothing but a providential interference, he decided, could have sent Zoeman, *hostile to Wenlock,* at that moment.

Why Zoeman had butted in, and why his obvious hostility to Wenlock, was a matter for conjecture – but not just then. He *had* butted in. Martin, a grin on his rugged face accepted Zoeman's mocking: 'You can come out, Storm,' with alacrity.

Zoeman, a revolver in his hand as steady as a rock, contrived to send a silent but comparatively friendly message. Behind him several youthful, clean-cut looking men whom Storm would have backed the world over to be Englishmen, peered towards Wenlock and his four gangsters.

Pedro was stretched out on the floor and from a hole in his forehead the blood oozed slowly and horribly. He was dead. The machine-gun lay upturned on the parquet flooring.

Wenlock hunted was a very different man from Wenlock hunting, but Zoeman cut across his shaking words.

'You never were much more than a bragging fool, Wenlock. Cut the cackle and get out. I'd kill you if I thought you were worth it, but you're not! Don't run away with the idea that you've got men in the grounds, because I've sent them all packing and I reckon those who aren't dead with fright are in that smart little garage you run. Get out!'

'But – ' began Wenlock, his face working convulsively. Storm had an idea that the man was afraid of something apart from the icy voice of Hesketh Zoeman.

Zoeman almost lost control of himself.

'Get out, damn you, get out! Or I'll plug you like I plugged Pedro!'

The bodyguard worked swiftly, and within five minutes were disappearing along the drive, forcing Wenlock and his men before them.

Storm looked gratefully towards Zoeman.

'Damn glad to see you,' he said warmly.

Zoeman smiled mockingly.

'I don't doubt it. When you get a little older, Storm, you'll know what to dabble with and what to leave alone. You're in a much more serious business than you can tackle. And don't run away with the idea that because I don't like Wenlock I'm head over heels in love with you. I'm not. To put it bluntly, you're making yourself a damned nuisance.'

'I like that!' breathed Storm indignantly. '*Me* making *myself* a damned nuisance! Listen, Zoeman. Young Granville invites me down here for a few days. I accept. I come. I get held up in the village, half-murdered here, on top of that the girl's been stolen – and you say I'm making myself a damned nuisance. Well – '

As he spoke he saw Zoeman's eyes narrow at mention of the girl, which meant that Zoeman knew nothing of the abduction. The mystery grew deeper. But the man with the mocking grin turned away from the subject.

'You men had better get a drink. And don't look at my gun as though it might go off. It won't – yet.'

Storm turned round, and as he turned caught sight of Granville's face. He went suddenly cold. He could have sworn that a veiled flash of mutual understanding passed between the owner of Ledsholm Grange and Zoeman!

Affecting to notice nothing he poured the whisky with a liberal hand, and toasted the rescue party.

'So,' said Zoeman sarcastically, 'it's all just an accident, is it?'

Storm smiled gently. The twins would come...

The older man went on: 'I've warned you once, Storm. Get out of this business and stay out. Don't make reports to anyone, because if you do, you'll be signing your own death warrant. Just fade away. You're fishing with a fly for tunny, and it won't work.'

'No?' queried Storm politely. 'Well – I'm devilish grateful for today, Zoeman. But I'm afraid I'm too deep in the stunt now to get out. You see' – he played with his cigarette case slowly – 'the little affair of Letty Granville holds my attention.'

'Supposing I undertake to release her?'

'It would be supposing,' grinned Storm. 'Until I told you, you didn't know that she had gone.'

'I have a certain influence with Wenlock,' said Zoeman grimly.

'Maybe,' acknowledged Storm. 'But I wouldn't be satisfied until I saw her. There's a lot of things about Wenlock that I don't like, but he's clever.'

Zoeman rubbed his chin.

'You're quicker than I thought,' he admitted grudgingly. 'All the same – you've got to drop out. Or be put out.'

Storm leaned forward.

'All the gunmen in Chicago,' he said earnestly, 'wouldn't make me drop out of this business now. Unless,' he added, 'one of them slugged me with lead.'

Zoeman's lips tightened.

'Up to now,' he said, 'I've been friendly. A few days ago I encountered one of your friends, a member of the famous "Z" Department. I hit him over the head,' went on Zoeman simply. 'I could have killed him as easily as I killed Pedro. As easily as I could have killed the two fools who belong to that Department and hang about Ledsholm with an idea that they're not known. As easily' – his voice went icily cold as he stared at Storm – 'as I could kill you.'

'I know, I know,' broke in Storm. 'Deep regrets and a gangster's funeral. Still – keep on trying.'

He was gazing past Zoeman towards the disused moat and the crumbling wall which surrounded Ledsholm Grange. A hundred yards along the drive, just in front of the shining Black Rock opposite the big drawbridge was something which interested him deeply, although no hint of what he had seen showed itself in his expression. He went on mildly:

'You see, Zoeman, I know that both you and Wenlock are pretty keen on getting possession of Ledsholm Grange. That gives me a certain advantage, for I know you'd hate to think that the police had any idea of this. So you'll naturally avoid doing anything which might attract their attention. Wenlock went off his rocker for a minute or he wouldn't have carried out the raid. So on the whole,' he added genially, 'it would be easier to clean Chicago of gunmen than clear me out of here. Kind of deadlock, isn't it?'

Zoeman fingered his gun.

'I had hoped,' he said dangerously, 'that you would see reason. All I want is Ledsholm Grange for a few weeks. But if I must put you out of action first – '

His automatic pointed directly at Storm. The latter, wise to the man's purpose, knew that he would be quite prepared to shoot; his ruthlessness shone from his piercing grey eyes.

But Storm was smiling easily. Zoeman's gun appeared to matter to him as little as a water pistol.

'I shouldn't try putting me out of action,' he said quietly. 'Your life wouldn't be worth much afterwards. I'd much rather give you the chance of leaving the neighbourhood.'

Zoeman stared at him uncertainly.

'What the devil – '

'Shhh!' exhorted Storm. 'Twenty yards behind you are six of the bonniest boys in all England, and each has a gun and each is looking at you without enthusiasm – '

Zoeman's eyes were mere silts.

'If you're fooling me, Storm – '

'I'm not,' said Storm, and the grimness of his voice carried conviction. 'Put your gun away or you'll catch a packet.' He waited for a moment, grinning mockingly into Zoeman's narrowed eyes before raising his voice, 'What-ho, Timothy! Hold your horses, old warrior.'

The plaintive voice of an immaculately-dressed young man wafted gently into the hall from the foot of the steps. The party of six young men merged together – they had separated in view of the possibility of gunfire – and on each face was a cheery grin.

'Well, old boy,' drawled Timothy Arran. 'Here we are, as merry as can be. You don't really mean that we've missed the show?'

Storm grinned.

'Only part of it. Walk right in and take a look,'

Zoeman viewed the six young men with amazement. They trooped into the hall, forming a wide circle round Zoeman and Storm as they broke into light-hearted banter.

'Be quiet,' broke in Storm, grinning. He had watched Zoeman carefully and felt himself warming towards the man as, after the first shock of surprise, his face creased into a smile. This is Zoeman. I don't know his other name so I can't tell you what it is. Anyhow, but for him you'd have been in time for the funeral.'

'Really,' said Timothy Arran apologetically, 'if we'd known we wouldn't have – I mean, honestly, we'd no idea that – '

'In spite of which,' said Storm, 'Zoeman is not one of us. In fact he's been making himself unpleasant.'

Timothy stared at him indignantly.

'Now look here, Windy, we really can't – I mean, first you tell us he is, and then you say he isn't.'

'And then,' interrupted Toby jerkily, 'you say he is again. What the blazes is the game? – '

'Remember that we came from London,' broke in the aggrieved voice of Dodo Trale, the fifth young man, 'especially for this stunt and at considerable – '

'Personal inconvenience,' finished Martin Best, the last member of the sextette, 'I might tell you, Windy, that I've a date with the second member of the third row at Daly's chorus.'

Storm turned to Zoeman, and there was no smile in his eyes.

'Now you've an idea,' he went on quietly, 'of the resources. There are others. But because of the way you potted Pedro I'm grateful.'

He saw the sudden eagerness in Zoeman's eyes and smiled to himself. He knew that Zoeman had his gun and he knew that Zoeman had heard the engine of a car which was turning into the drive, manned by three of his own gunmen who had routed Wenlock.

But Storm realised that Zoeman could never be forced to talk. Zoeman free was more likely to yield results than Zoeman captured.

He did nothing as the older man darted backwards, bringing his gun into sight in a flash that rivalled lightning.

'You're asking for it, Storm. I've done all I could. I can't help you again. Take my tip and call your men off.'

Zoeman stared round him. Not one of the six newcomers nor the trio which he had rescued moved an inch nor made the slightest effort to reach a gun. He felt that in Storm he had met a man whose methods and ability were beyond him, and for a moment the thought made him uneasy.

But whatever else, he was going to get away. The three men outside in the car were already showing their guns, and only Zoeman's left hand raised high above his head stopped them from shooting. He knew better than to try conclusions at that moment with Storm and his men. Retreat was the only choice, and he retreated, confused by the utter immobility of the men in the hall.

Then Storm stepped forward.

'You can put your gun away,' he said affably. 'As you've got so far I won't stop you going further. But' – there was a grimness about his mouth which brought a corresponding hardness to Zoeman's lips – 'next time we'll take the gloves off, Zoeman. I'm in possession – meaning that Granville's in possession with me to help him – and I'm going to keep it that way. So gloves off, next time. Suit you?'

Zoeman nodded slowly.

'Perfectly,' he said quietly, and to Storm's satisfaction put his gun in his pocket.

Whatever else, Zoeman would fight clean.

Storm saw the other looking askance at the short, podgy little man who suddenly swung into the drive at the wheel of a decrepit-looking Morris two-seater. He grinned, raising his voice so that the men waiting in the Frazer Nash at the foot of the steps, Zoeman's men, heard him.

'He's all right, sonnies. It's our caretaker cove.'

Harries, returning from his trip into Ledsholm for viands, was driving dejectedly. The back of the car was full of parcels and packages, and Harries was not looking forward to the amount of cooking that would have to be done.

Storm grinned at the thought of the henchman's dismay when he found another six young men added to the dinner list, but as he watched the slowly moving Morris, whose driver stared curiously at Zoeman and the Frazer Nash as it passed him, he went suddenly cold.

One moment Harries was driving carelessly but with complete control of the small car. The next he was lolling forward over the steering wheel, the Morris rearing up like a great crab on its back wheels.

But there had been something horrible in the expression on the caretaker's face as he lolled forward, something which froze the blood in Storm's veins.

Harries was dead! Even at that distance Storm saw the spreading red horror of a wound in the centre of his forehead!

10

NEWS OF LETTY GRANVILLE

'It wasn't Zoeman,' said Storm with an icy calm. 'I had him in full view all the time. It was someone from the right, and I've an idea that I saw them dodge down from the wall as I looked over.' He laid a steadying hand on Granville's arm. 'Steady, young fellow. Probably a doctor will help.'

'Doctor nothing!' rasped Granville savagely. 'He's dead, you know it as well as I do!'

Storm shrugged his shoulders hopelessly, and was glad when Timothy Arran handed Granville a stiff peg of whisky. As the younger man gulped it down a vestige of colour returned to his pale cheeks.

He gave a short laugh.

'I'm sorry. I didn't think it would be as bad as this. But I brought you into it – '

'Oh no you didn't,' broke in Storm decisively. 'I was already in.'

He swung round on Timothy Arran abruptly.

'Tim – do you still know the daughter of the Assistant P.M.G.?'

Timothy nodded, although he could see no connection between the sudden, cold-blooded murder and the pretty brunette daughter of the Assistant Postmaster General.

'Good,' he grunted. 'Get through to her and ask her if she'll pull the strings and find out who subscribes to Mayfair one-eight-double-ought-nine. Tell her it's a joke – but get the name and address.'

Mystified but eager to help, Timothy put a toll call through to London and within ten minutes was chatting away as if he hadn't a serious thought in the world. Miss Felicity du Corle had not the slightest idea but that the telephone inquiry was an afterthought. Viewing Timothy Arran with some favour she promised to do her best.

Meanwhile, the body of the unfortunate Harries had been carried into one of the upstairs rooms, and Granville was talking somewhere at the back of the house with Mrs Harries. It was a devilish business – and Storm knew that the only counter was action and quick action.

The telephone bell burred out within fifteen minutes and Timothy picked up the receiver. He scribbled down something as he murmured gaily into the mouthpiece, then hung up with every show of reluctance.

'Got it?' demanded Storm.

'Love us, of course I have,' drawled Timothy. 'Here we are. Mr Sommers Lee-Knight, 19 Park Street, Mayfair, London.'

'Good chap,' approved Storm. 'Now – which of you boys want a trip to town and who wants to stay here?' He looked round. 'Tim, you and Toby had better come with me – and you, Granville. Grimy, keep an eye on these lunatics, don't let them wander far and watch like blazes for the Wenlock crowd. Zoeman's too, for that matter. All clear?'

'What's the stunt?' demanded Grimm.

'Mayfair 18009,' said Storm, 'is the number which the bright boy in the telephone box tried to get. There's a sound chance that the cove was too scared to tell Wenlock that he let it slip. They're probably holding Letty there – '

Less than ten minutes afterwards Storm, Granville and the twins were clambering into a roomy Bugatti roadster, Timothy Arran driving.

During the journey Storm managed to work out the affairs of the afternoon.

In the first place the attacking party against Ledsholm Grange had split in two – unless there had always been two. It was well on the boards that Zoeman, in the first interview, had deliberately made him, Storm, think that he was working the London operations for Redhead. Whether or no, Wenlock – if he was Redhead – and Zoeman were bitter antagonists, Storm had little hesitation in putting his money on Zoeman.

From that point he came to the inevitable problem. Why were Wenlock and Zoeman dead keen on getting possession of Ledsholm Grange?

He didn't know. But he licked his lips as he determined that he would know before the murderous business was over.

Another point which eased his mind was that Wenlock's interest was in the Grange itself and not, as Storm had at first imagined, chiefly in Letty Granville.

Less satisfactory was the murder of Harries. Little though he had seen of the dour old servant he had every reason to believe that the trust which Granville had reposed in him was fully justified. Storm realised in spite of this that the murderers – Wenlock's men without a shadow of doubt – had an idea that Harries might have been able to tell something which would have led to complications.

Ledsholm Grange held a secret. What was it?

From that unanswerable query he went to the disturbing problem of the dead Harries. There were ways of hiding a live man, but keeping a dead body without reporting it to the authorities was liable to lead to trouble. He ought to report.

But that would bring a small army of police as well as newspaper men to the Grange, and he was frankly afraid of going to the police. He knew enough now of the cold-blooded devilishness of the gangsters, enough to be sure that if he 'squeaked' it would be signing his own death warrant as well as those of the twins and their bodyguard, and the Granvilles. Police or no police, Redhead would get them.

Storm felt a chilling horror at the man's overpowering lust for vengeance.

He looked forward eagerly to the call on Mr Sommer Lee-Knight. It was becoming increasingly urgent to trace Letty and he felt in his bones that the house of Mr Lee-Knight was likely to prove interesting.

Park Street turned out to be one of those extremely narrow thoroughfares set with gloomy stone houses towering five or six storeys high. At the identical moment that Timothy Arran swung his wheel round to turn into it, a gigantic Delage poked its nose towards the main road.

Timothy swerved, forcing the Bugatti on the pavement and bringing it to rest within an inch of a massive lamp standard.

Cool and unperturbed, he looked at the Delage and then launched into a mild grouse against the chauffeur's original way of coming out of a side street. The man had at least the grace to look shaken, but the old man huddled up in the back seat showed no sign whatever of rage, fright or injury.

Storm's voice hissed in Timothy's ear.

'Make the blighter wait for you, Tim, then let him get clear and follow.'

'I mean,' continued Timothy plaintively, 'I'm in the deuce of a hurry. So if you don't mind I'll – thanks a lot.'

The liveried chauffeur had by now recovered his nerve and lost his temper. Knowing the signs Timothy was prepared for a stream of Cockney invective, but Storm, knowing more, was waiting for the nasal tirade typical of the Bowery toughs.

He would have staked his life on the chauffeur being one of Wenlock's gunmen!

But both Timothy and Martin were surprised. The huddled figure inside the Delage moved at last. Leaning out of the window his voice came, rasping with authority.

'Be quiet, Vines. The fault was yours. Wait.'

Timothy waved a carefree hand but Storm was leaning back in the car, strangely cold, chilled by the man's green eyes!

A brief line of hair beneath the hat was surely red?

He might have been an older edition of Wenlock himself!

But was he older? Those green eyes had glowed with all the fervour of youth. The car, dark and roomy, was an admirable shelter for a man to assume an effective and admirable disguise.

Thankfully Storm realised that there was a sound chance that neither he nor Granville had been seen. They were sitting low in the car behind the twins, and neither the man in the back nor the driver could see through flesh and bone.

In a trice two alternatives flashed through Storm's mind. If he could get news of Letty Granville from the Park Street house it would be crazy to chase after the Delage. On the other hand, if the seeming ancient was Wenlock it was odds on a better reward coming from pursuit. His whisper to Timothy Arran told of his decision.

Timothy had espied an opening twenty yards down the road. By the time he had reached it and turned his car the Delage was on the move.

'After it!' snapped Storm.

The Bugatti snorted and lurched to the main road. Storm gritted his teeth as it narrowly missed the standard and, with that mad exhilaration for the chase surging through his blood, grinned round at Granville.

But the younger man seemed to have gone mad. Heedless of the racing car he stood up, waving frantically to something on the right side of the road. His face was livid with excitement as he swung round on Storm.

'Stop! Letty's there! *I saw her!*'

Storm's grin faded as he touched Timothy's hunched shoulder.

'Whoa, Tim! Stop her, boy!'

The big car pulled up dead a couple of yards from the end of the road. Arran turned furiously.

'What the blazes are you tishying about? Do you want me to stop or do you want me to – '

The next thing the indignant Timothy saw was the massive figure of Martin Storm and the smaller one of Granville hurtling across the road. Timothy gathered, with Tobias, that something was up. Grabbing their guns but careful to keep them out of sight they brought up the rear after backing the Bugatti to a safer parking place.

Outside number nineteen Storm was waiting for them.

The girl,' said Storm simply, 'is up there. Granville saw her. I saw her.'

'Hump,' grunted Toby. 'What now?'

'Let's get at that door.'

On the surface of things it was crazy, but none knew more than Martin Storm the need for speed and the probability of a bold stroke coming off. There were many ways that Wenlock and his thugs might expect them to force an entry; knocking at the front door was most unlikely to be one of them.

With one hand in his pocket around the butt of his gun he took a firm hold on the knocker with the other.

His rat-tat-tat thundered along the narrow street. Once – twice – thrice. Then:

'They're moving,' he muttered.

He sensed the excitement consuming Granville and felt his own heart thumping against his ribs. A moment later he heard someone fumbling with the latch and his grip on his gun tightened.

The door opened.

The ancient standing there might have been a hundred. Wizened, yellow-faced, wrinkled by many criss-cross lines, a sharp-featured, piercing-eyed old harridan confronted them. Her voice was harsh and querulous.

'What do you want?'

'Hum,' mumbled Storm, 'this rather alters matters.'

'What? What's that?'

'Sorry,' murmured Storm. 'I was wondering whether a friend of mine – '

'No!' said the harridan with acid finality. 'No friends of yours are here. Good-day.'

Storm saw the sudden cattish fury on the lined face as he inserted his foot in the doorway.

Her expression quickly changed as he showed his gun.

'Where is she?' he asked sharply.

With some regrets he let Granville push open the door to which the old woman sulkily led them, opening it with a key taken from a massive bunch. Adroitly Storm took the keys from her and dropped them into his own pocket.

She swore at him, almost spitting in her rage. Very gently Storm lifted her from the floor and heedless of her struggles, carried her to the nearest room. Opening the door he deposited her therein, kissed his hand airily and, making early use of the bunch of keys, locked the door.

'Lord, Windy,' murmured Timothy, 'what a let down! Here we are all ready for stink bombs and battle-axes, and we get a reincarnated mummy and one beauteous damsel in – '

'Not so much of the beauteous damsel,' growled Storm, looking towards the door on the third floor behind which Granville had disappeared. The handle turned suddenly and Granville's face appeared, wreathed in smiles.

'Sling me your mackintosh, Storm, will you? Good man. Thanks. Half a mo'.'

Letty was obviously all right apart from the little matter of apparel, and the thought cheered Storm's susceptible heart. He had ample opportunity, three minutes later, of seeing for himself.

He leapt forward.

'How are you?' he demanded.

'Thanks to you,' she said quietly, 'I'm all right.'

'No damage?'

'Only talk and more talk,' answered Letty, and from the shudder which ran through her slight frame he gathered that Wenlock had used all his devilish ingenuity to scare her. Shadows beneath her eyes and a nervousness which she tried unsuccessfully to hide, told its own tale.

Storm's heart seethed, but he forgot Wenlock for a moment in realising that she presented an immediate and urgent problem. To take her back to Ledsholm was unthinkable. No, they had to find somewhere in London, somewhere that he could be sure she was safe.

So far, thought Storm, so good. Wenlock might be thinking that even if the attack on the Grange had failed he still had the girl, but Wenlock would soon find that his card had been trumped.

He grinned at the twins, who were leading the way down the stairs. Toby Arran had reached the bottom step ahead of the others when the front door was flung open.

Toby's hand slipped to his hip pocket but he didn't touch his gun.

On the threshold stood Ralph Wenlock!

The gleaming gun in his hand was pointed unwaveringly at the party on the stairs, and his fanatical green eyes, glowing with all-consuming hatred, seemed to burn into them.

He took a step forward, exposing the four brutal faces of the roughneck members of his gang who were behind him. Above him, spread out along the stairs so that they made a perfect mark even for an indifferent marksman, were Storm, Frank Granville, Letty and the twins.

Storm's blood ran cold.

11

A GETAWAY AND SOME DISCOVERIES

Wenlock's green eyes stared malevolently at Storm.
Into the minds of all four men on the stairs the
same thought had sent the same dismay. One false move
would be enough to make Wenlock fire at the girl. No matter how quickly they moved, Wenlock's bullet, biting devilishly from the gun which was levelled at her heart, would
start its hum of death.

Storm's brow was wet and his face grim. The situation
was desperate. Then, dropping into that simulation of careful geniality which cloaked the hard purposefulness of his
mind he grinned.

'What-ho, Wenlock. How we do keep bumping into each
other!'

Wenlock snarled: 'Keep quiet, Storm. Seltzer!' He spoke
over his shoulder. 'Get their guns.'

Storm could hardly believe his ears. Wenlock was giving him the one chance that he needed to make a fight, the
chance which they had not had at the Grange. Defying armed

men at ten yards distance was suicidal; trying it when one of them was near enough to be grappled was a different matter.

Not for the first time Storm had a vague doubt about Wenlock. The gang which he led, the fear which he inspired in America as well as England, seemed to emanate from a personality a hundred times stronger than Wenlock's. The red-haired man in front of him was evil, but he seemed to lack strength.

Was Wenlock Redhead?

The twins, standing motionless, sensed the opportunity as well as Storm and were in a better position to make use of it. Timothy was in front of the girl, with her brother and Storm behind. More gentle than cooing doves the twins, with studious regard for the guns gleaming in the hands of the men just inside the door, allowed Seltzer to give them the onceover. Two automatics slipped into Seltzer's pocket.

The gangster leered into the face of the girl. With an irrepressible shudder of revulsion at the brutal, unclean stare, Letty backed towards the bannisters.

Seltzer's thick lips parted in a guttural laugh, but Wenlock's voice cut across it.

'Get to it, Seltzer!'

'Exactly,' murmured Timothy Arran. Then: 'Duck!' he bawled madly.

As he bellowed he swung round like a miniature cyclone. Seltzer, secure in the thought of the guns supporting him, was unprepared. He found his left arm twisted excruciatingly and he stared into the wicked green eyes of Wenlock as he was swung round so that his fleshy body gave the party on the stairs good cover.

As Timothy moved, Storm shot out two massive arms, thrusting Letty down so quickly that any shot Wenlock might have chanced would miss her.

But Wenlock's gun was silent. For a moment he was nonplussed by the whirlwind speed of the manoeuvre, and for the fatal fraction of time which mattered he hesitated to use his gun for fear of hitting Seltzer. Before he decided to chance it, the gangster was flung bodily at him. Wenlock staggered back, crashing into the men behind him. A struggling, cursing heap made up all that was left of the attacking party for the precious minute that Storm and the twins wanted.

Storm's gun was in his hand as he leapt downwards, kicking ruthlessly at Wenlock's wrist as the latter tried to train his gun. It went flying out of his numbed hand.

'Our turn,' grunted Storm.

Diving downwards he grabbed at the guns from the struggling gangsters. Seltzer, winded and bruised, yielded up those he had taken from the twins as well as his own.

There were many things which Storm would have liked to have done, including a comprehensive search of Number 19, Park Street, but with the girl on their hands and the possibility of reinforcements arriving at any moment, discretion was called for. With the help of the twins he bundled Wenlock and his thugs inside a nearby room and locked it. Heedless of the red-haired man's stream of blasphemies wafted to him through the keyhole, he flung open the front door.

Timothy Arran was out in a flash. Within sixty seconds the Bugatti was backed outside the house and Letty carried out and deposited within.

Storm's mind was working at top speed. He had to get the girl away and he wanted to be back in time to make a complete search of the house. That meant two of them staying behind to keep an eye on Wenlock and the prisoners.

Timothy Arran, his fingers on the wheel, felt Storm's hand on his shoulder.

'Get back inside, Tim, will you? Hold them there until we get back. Bust out if any extras come along and drop in at the *Carilon Club*. Toby'll keep outside and if there's anything that looks like trouble he'll give you a shout. I'll handle the car.'

Timothy hated, more than anything else in the world, letting the car out of his hands, but for the time being Storm was handling affairs. He slipped out of the driver's seat.

'How long'll you be?'

'Half-an-hour at the outside.'

As Storm swung the Bugatti round the corner of Park Street he grinned cheerfully round at Letty, whose white face lifted in a smile.

'Now we won't be long,' he managed over his shoulder. 'I'm running you round to some friends – stout folk who'll ask no questions.'

As the great car swung into Philmore Crescent Martin Storm looked as cool and collected a young man as existed in London. Not even the shrewdest member of the C.I.D. would have imagined that he had faced death three times during that hectic day.

A stately and slightly disapproving man-servant opened the front door. If he was outraged at the sight of the two men and the weary, tousled girl clad from head to foot in a gigantic mackintosh he gave no sign.

Summoned, Sir Joseph and Lady Grimm greeted them pleasantly. They were used, and fairly tolerant, of the unorthodox adventures of their son and his cousin.

'Sorry,' explained Storm cheerfully, 'but I'm in a bit of a fix. One damsel is in need of shelter and sustenance. Haven't time now, or I'd give you the yarn. D'you mind?'

'All the same if we do,' grumbled Sir Joseph good-humouredly. 'Well, bring her in, my boy.'

But Sir Joseph had hardly started to speak before the kindly and attractive Lady Alicia was in the hall.

Storm smiled. The two women would get on well.

He waved thanks and an airy farewell, his eyes holding Letty's with an unspoken promise of many things to say and many more to happen. Then he turned to Granville. 'Coming or staying?'

'Coming,' said Granville without hesitation.

Storm saw the sudden flash of fear in Letty's eyes, but she fought it back. He felt ridiculously light-hearted. They were the goods, the Granvilles!

For the moment that lurking doubt at the back of his mind concerning Frank was forgotten.

They were back at Park Street well within his half-an-hour time limit, and he breathed a sigh of satisfaction when he saw Toby Arran standing beneath a lamp post lighting a cigarette.

'All clear,' he said as the Bugatti drew up. 'And from what I can gather, one of the boys in the parlour got nasty, and Timothy improved the shining hour by swiping him one. There was noise but little else.'

'Seen him since the shindy?' demanded Storm.

'Yes,' said Tobias with unkind humour. 'Difficult not to, with that black eye!'

'But it was worth it,' said Timothy, when Storm confronted him. 'Better put a rope round 'em, Martin. There's some in the car.'

Exactly a quarter-of-an-hour later the four men closed the front door of Number 19, Park Street, and clambered into the Bugatti. The whole house had been ransacked for information, but little had been forthcoming beyond the fact that Mr Sommers Lee-Knight was an eminently respectable barrister who was honeymooning abroad and had let his house for six months to a gentleman named Gazzoni.

The name Gazzoni was interesting, but not informative. They hoped that it was the beginning of greater things. For the time being they had been in the house as long as wisdom suggested, for if another batch of Wenlock's thugs arrived it was unlikely that they would get away with it as easily.

With some justification the twins believed that Wenlock should be carted away with them. He would probably talk. And, they said, if he was the Big Boy of the party operations from the gangsters would be nil.

'I have very serious doubts,' said Storm reflectively, 'whether Wenlock *is* Redhead. In any case, my reasoning is that if we cart Wenlock away with us the others will start a counterattack at the Grange, and for the time being we could do with a few hours for looking round. There's a lot of things about Ledsholm Grange that might prove interesting.'

'But,' protested Tobias, 'big fish lead to bigger fish. If we take Wenlock with us –'

'Wenlock'll do us more good here than at the Grange,' reasoned Storm. 'We can afford to wait for their next move, and while we're waiting we can look around the Grange. What we want more than anything else is breathing space, and now we've got the girl back we've nothing to worry about but our own skins.'

'I suppose you're right,' admitted Tobias dubiously.

'Step on it,' grinned Storm. 'If you hurry there'll just be time for one at the *Carilon*.'

Arriving at the *Carilon*, Storm wrote a brief but urgent note to Sir Joseph and Lady Alicia Grimm. He was wide-awake to the possibility of their having been followed from Ledsholm by some of Zoeman's men, and he wanted to make sure that the knight viewed his new charge with due importance. It had been impossible to talk too much in front of the Granvilles.

It's just possible, he wrote, that an attempt will be made to get Miss Granville out of the house by her-self. Please take no notice of anything or anybody but Roger or myself, in person. And it might be as well to keep an eye on gas-fitters and electric-light johnnies. Sorry and all that.

It was just after midnight that the Bugatti swung round by Black Rock and hummed over the disused drawbridge. As they caught sight of the mansion Storm realised more keenly than ever the loneliness of the Grange, and its per-fect suitability for criminal enterprises.

Every possible light in the house was now blazing. Grimm had reduced the chances of a surprise attack under cover of darkness to a minimum.

He greeted them exuberantly, and the success of their sortie was passed on with admirable brevity and considerable enthusiasm. They felt that the first trick had been turned to their favour, and there followed a hectic and entirely ami-able set-to, in the course of which the best part of a tankard of beer was poured over Storm's trousers.

'Darn you!' he exploded, viewing the agent of destruc-tion – the large and untidy Martin Best, now doubled up with laughter. 'That's the kind of senseless horseplay you would shine in. Look at my trousers!'

'I am looking,' stuttered Best.

Storm was realising that beer soaking into one's nether garments was not only sartorially ruinous, it was cold. He had just reached the point of remembering that he had left his heavy cases behind him, and carried not even a spare pair of breeks, when a mournful voice broke into his gloom.

'Your blue, sir, or your grey? I brought – '

Storm leapt into the air with relief.

'Horrors,' he said emphatically, 'believe me, I'll lend you half-a-crown one day. Grey, boy, and quickly. When did you arrive?'

'By the eight-twenty train.'

'Poor devil had to walk,' grinned Righteous Dane. 'That wall-eyed cab horse in the village rolled over when he saw the bags.'

'You *walked?*' queried Storm.

'Unfortunately yes, sir. It wouldn't budge – the horse I mean. So – '

'Go to bed,' grinned Storm. 'I'll get my own trousers.'

At one o'clock, reclad and happily demolishing cheese and biscuits, Storm and the other members of the company discussed affairs with considerable verve. The rescue of the girl had put new blood in their veins and a mild murmur from Grimm to the effect that it might be wise to make a call at Whitehall was cried down.

There was some justification for their attitude. Storm saw the move as asking for trouble while Redhead was still at large. As soon as they could make sure of getting Redhead and, possibly, Zoeman, they would chat readily enough with the Men Who Mattered. But not before.

Nothing had happened to disturb the peace of Ledsholm Grange since the murder of Harries, suggesting that Zoeman had followed Wenlock out of the neighbourhood. But they could not count on this.

Although every door apart from that in the main hall had been locked and every window shuttered and barred, the task of making sure that there was no forced entry was as near impossible as made no difference. Storm, who had secured a rough plan of the Grange earlier in the day, drafted out a scheme for defence. It might be needed only for one night, but one night might be enough to put paid to their earthly accounts.

Ignoring the existence of the two upper storeys he concentrated on the ground floor. The servants' quarters, now occupied by the two gardeners only – Mrs Harries having gone to relatives until such time as Mr Frank wanted her again – and Horrobin, were to be shut off entirely from the main hall. The stairs leading to the upper part of the house were reached through the passages dividing the main hall from the servants' quarters.

Against the doors leading to the west wing and those of the upstairs rooms a barricade of furniture was erected speedily and solidly by the energetic bodyguard.

In the words of Storm the east wing was occupied by the main army. It comprised four sizeable rooms, including a dining-room and an extensive library, and two which were utilised as bedrooms.

The chapel, which Granville told them had not been opened for five years, was connected with the east wing by a small passage, while the electrical plant was installed in a brick-built shed adjoining the servants quarters in the courtyard at the back of the Grange.

Weary-eyed as the first streaks of dawn began to force their way across the skies, Storm looked across at the others.

'There's some talk of underground passages, Granny. Know anything about them?'

Granville managed a weary smile.

'There's a cellar, of course; the door just behind the hall leads to it, but apart from that they're fairy tales.'

'What's that about fairy tales?' murmured Martin Best, waking up suddenly.

'There passed a whole day when you didn't talk,' Storm told him. 'Go back to sleep, Nosey.'

He stood up, stretching his arms.

'I'm going to turn in, you fellows. Roger – you've been asleep longer than anybody, keep awake until seven and make Best stay with you. Then you'd better call Righteous and Dodo. They can dig the twins out at nine.'

'What about you?' demanded St John Dane aggrievedly.

'I,' said Storm sweetly, 'do the brainwork, Righteous. I need more sleep. Chin-chin, chaps!'

But Storm was fated to one completely sleepless night. As he stepped across the door leading to the newly-made bedrooms the light from the great hanging chandelier flickered.

Then the room was swallowed in a black cloud!

No one spoke. The darkness seemed to demand silence.

After a full thirty seconds Timothy Arran's plaintive voice disturbed the heavy silence, but his second word was hardly out of his mouth when he stopped as though struck by a knife!

From somewhere at the back of the Grange came a long, eerie, blood-curdling scream, a scream of human terror, a scream which froze the very blood in their veins as it screeched through the black silence.

12

Mr Benjamin Cripps Confides

As the last vibration of that terrible shriek died away, Storm's voice, no more than a whisper but plainly audible through the great hall, sighed through the unnerving darkness.

'Have any of you men got a torch?'

Two voices, ghosts of their real selves but emphatic enough, answered affirmatively.

'Trust me,' asserted the easy-going Martin Best, whose casual attention to his clothes was more than countered by his general usefulness in filling his pockets with a host of gadgets likely to 'come in handy some time'.

'Call here,' murmured Timothy Arran.

'You stay where you are, Tim,' said Storm quickly, shaking off the effect of that ghastly cry. 'Granville, you come with me. Righteous and Best'll come too. The others will stay with Tim, and for heaven's sake keep your ears open and your eyes peeled. There's an outside chance that it's a stunt to get us all to the back of the house.'

With the bright beam of Martin Best's torch to guide them Storm, Granville, Dane, and Best moved towards the servants quarters. The eeriness of the great hall, the sudden change from brilliance to abysmal darkness and the awful, quivering horror of that one cry gave them all a chilled uncertainty as they moved.

The white moon of the light shone on the handle of the door leading to the passage in front of the servants quarters. Storm turned it softly and stepped into the gloom, followed quickly by the others, their cold hands gripping the steel of their guns.

Storm tried the wall-switch in the large, bare kitchen, but nothing happened.

'The main switch has gone,' muttered Best, the only one likely to have sufficient technical knowledge to put the trouble right – always providing the trouble was accidental; the possibility of intentional damage loomed uncomfortably large.

But who had sent that terror-stricken cry quivering through the night?

'Better go straight to the electric plant,' said Storm as they stepped towards the door leading into the courtyard. 'Do you keep it locked, Granville?'

'I don't know,' muttered Granville, keeping his voice steady with an effort. 'Smithers, the under-gardener, looks after it.'

As Storm unlocked the kitchen door, all of them were chillingly aware that somewhere beyond them would be the explanation of that awful shriek. What was it? Who was it?

The courtyard, lit with the eerie grey streaks of dawn, shewed bare and clean as they stepped on to the flagstones, turning towards the small, brick-built shed which sheltered the dynamo and electric plant of the Grange. Best switched off his light.

'The door's open,' muttered Righteous Dane.

Storm went first, taking the torch from Best. As he directed the sudden stream of brilliant white light towards the inside of the shed his lips tightened and the glint in his eyes was like steel.

Sprawling across the floor of the power-house was the horribly twisted body of a man, a man dressed in a suit of pyjamas which was revealed by the open folds of a great-coat obviously flung round him as he had left his bedroom in some emergency and alarm.

That he was dead, there wasn't a shadow of doubt. As Storm peered down into the distorted face he felt a surge of rage run through his veins.

The bloodless lips were drawn back over bared teeth in a ghastly snarl, and the features were twisted almost beyond recognition. The eyes, staring horribly from their sockets, shewed such fear of the agonising death which had struck him that a shivering wave of nausea gripped Storm's stomach. He reached out his hand to touch him.

'Stop!' roared Best. He gave a grim, mirthless smile.

'The poor devil's been electrocuted. If he's still touching the live point you'd get a nasty shock.' He looked round the small power house quickly, grunting with satisfaction as he pounced on a pair of rubber gloves.

He drew them on, then kneeling by that terribly distorted body, gently turned the man over. Granville cursed between his teeth.

'Recognise him?' demanded Storm.

Granville nodded, white to the lips.

'It's Smithers. God! This is ghastly.'

They waited for a minute while Best searched the body for the mark of burning. He found it across the palm of the right hand.

'Touched the control switch,' vouchsafed Best without hesitation. 'It can be done but it's not safe to try it without gloves. I reckon he slipped and made a circuit.'

'So it might have been accidental?'

'It probably was,' admitted Best. Then grimly: 'But that wasn't.'

He pointed to a contact-bar and plate which had been smashed and dented into a shapeless mass of metal. The brief hope that Storm had held passed; the death of Smithers might have been accidental, but beyond a shadow of doubt someone had been in the grounds apart from the gardener, someone who had not only wanted the lights put out but had meant to make a repair impossible without several hours' work.

Twenty minutes later the twisted body of Smithers was lying in a room which already contained the murdered Harries. Perriman, the head-gardener, shaken and white-faced, told them that Smithers had remembered that the safety catches had not been put on, and that he had gone to the power-house to make sure no damage was caused.

'How long ago?' demanded Storm.

'Mebbe an hour, sir, mebbe not so long.'

'Hump,' murmured Storm. 'Well, we'll have to have the police in, now. How d' you feel?' he queried.

'I feel shaken, sir. That's two in one day.'

'Make sure you don't move without Horrobin,' said Storm quietly. 'It's safest. Later in the morning we'll see what can be done. Fit enough to carry on for a bit?'

'I'll manage, sir, thank ye.'

Twenty minutes later the full party of eight was in the large hall, infinitely more aware of the horror of the thing against which they were pitting themselves. It was

Storm who voiced the general sentiments as he repeated soberly:

'We'll have to tell the police, you men. It's gone too far.'

There was a short silence of reluctant consent.

'I'll write to the great Sir William Divot,' enlarged Storm. 'He'll get the letter tomorrow morning, leaving us another full day to work.'

'Still think it might have been murder?' demanded Grimm.

'Shouldn't wonder,' admitted Storm. 'I've a nasty idea that the servants might know more than they said they did, and that they're getting bumped off to make sure that they don't talk.' He put a friendly arm along Granville's shoulder. 'The next thing is a little chat with Perriman now that he's steadied down a bit.'

But he met with another rebuff when he reached the large kitchen. Only Horrobin was there. The expression of uneasy relief on his chubby face made Storm more keenly aware of the creepy atmosphere of fear at Ledsholm Grange.

There was more than enough excuse for it. Two deaths, both brutal and unexplained, a pitched battle and the preparations for a seige were enough to give any normal, life-loving human the willies.

'What-ho!' greeted Storm with cheering intent. 'Seen Perriman, Horrors?'

'You mean the head gardener?' queried Horrobin, trying to make amends for his jumpiness with fastidious exactitude. 'He left less than five minutes ago, sir.'

'Say where he was going?' demanded Storm abruptly.

'No sir. Just said he wouldn't be long.'

'Did he, indeed,' snapped Storm. 'Grab anything you want and get into the front of the house with the others, and don't go anywhere about the house by yourself. Hurry!'

Horrobin gathered his few belongings together with admirable celerity. He had been jumpy and nervous, and the prospect of staying alone in the great, bare kitchen had not cheered him.

The party in the hall was subdued, but jerked into action as Storm clattered towards the door.

He said abruptly: 'Perriman has deserted. It's plenty light enough now. Travel in twos, you men, and bring him in somehow.'

But Perriman had vanished completely from the face of the earth. There was not the remotest possibility of his having made his way on foot, for the country around was bare and comparatively low-lying.

Storm's question was whether it was desertion or abduction. He could have understood the former and he feared the latter. But one fact stood out starkly.

Zoeman or Wenlock had a hiding place somewhere near the Grange itself!

'Pipped,' mourned Timothy Arran plaintively. 'I knew we were making a hash of things when we let Wenlock go, Windy. Really, if only you'd done – '

'What I told you,' mimicked Storm with ill-humour, 'we'd have been blown out of Sussex by now.'

He meant what he said: that until Redhead's gang was rounded up there was the possibility of a bullet spitting out from any corner. In spite of his faith in the discretion of Sir Joseph Grimm, he was also worried about Letty. Added to the murders at the Grange these fears were making him irritable.

He spoke quickly to Toby Arran.

'Trot round to the garage, Toby, and get the Bug out before I knock this blithering idiot's head off.'

'Whaffor?' demanded Toby.

'A trip to the village, no less. And you're not coming with me. I've another little game for you to play.'

'And that is?'

'A search for secret passages,' said Storm. 'All of you tap the walls in every room we're using. You might find some part hollow. I've a nasty idea that we're sitting on top of a mine, and I don't want it to go off.'

During the ten minute run into Ledsholm village, Storm was deciding on his next step. He intended to send a brief and uninformative note to the Assistant Secretary from the post office, knowing that he would have a full twenty-four hours to work out his own plans. But would Wenlock and Zoeman show up within a day? And what, if they didn't, would be the consequences of reporting to the police?

He was fully aware of the danger which threatened from Redhead. But whatever the Home Office and the police thought, he was in the affair to the end, if only to make sure that Letty Granville was clear of danger.

The first place Storm called at was the *Four Bells*. Here he was received with a welcoming smile by Benjamin Cripps, for Storm was a nine days' wonder in the village to all but the local constable, who viewed the interference from – said rumour – Scotland Yard resentfully but without open protest. For it had happened several years before that P.C. Gummer had been very severely censured for interfering with C.T.D. work. In consequence, frigid with disapproval, he made nothing but his customary daily report to the Lewes headquarters, and as he had not learned of the outrage at the post office until that very morning, Lewes knew nothing of it until the following day.

Once in the cosy hostelry, Timothy Arran and Storm immediately buried their noses in tankards of beer.

'Here's your very good heath, Mr Cripps. More like weather today, what?'

'Ye're right, sir,' acknowledged Benjamin heartily. 'Be ye likely to stay hereabouts for long, sir?'

Storm shrugged his shoulders.

'It all depends – ' He leaned forward, lowering his voice to confidential undertones, very thrilling to the amateur detective secreted within the innermost heart of mine host. 'It all depends on whether I can get the information I want, Mr Cripps.'

'If I can help – ' breathed Benjamin.

'Splendid,' whispered Storm. 'Now – have there been any strangers around lately, Mr Cripps? Apart from those two vagabonds we caught yesterday?'

Benjamin adopted an owlish expression of deep thought.

'Well, sir, there have and there haven't, in a manner of speaking. Mr Granville knows all about it, so maybe he could tell ye more.'

'You make a start, anyhow,' said Storm, concealing his surprise. Granville knew strangers, did he? The possibility staggered him, bringing the doubts he had once harboured back in full force.

'It's that there wireless thingummy,' said Benjamin. 'Not that I've any objection to wireless, sir, but they do say that Mr Granville is having what you might call a set that sends out. Trans – something or other.'

'Transmitting station,' supplied Storm, flabbergasted.

'That's the word, sir!' Mr Cripps viewed his detective client with deepening respect. 'Well, there's been a goodly number of men building the station, sir, at the back of the Grange – underneath it, they say. Mebbe ye've seen it. Love-a-duck! The loads o' thingummies they did have to make it with! They might have been building another house, what with bricks and rubber and steel – '

'How long ago was this?' demanded Storm.

'A week, sir, was the time I last saw them, though they were about the Grange for a month or more. Old Tom Harries – ye'll know him, sir, up at the house – was only talking to me about it yester morn. He asked me, if ye'll excuse me saying so, sir, not to let on to Mr Granville that I knew about it.' Mine host delivered himself of an expressive wink. 'Mr Granville, ye'll understand, was going to have it as a surprise for Miss Letty, and Harries shouldn't 'ave told me about it. But Tom and I being pally it kind of got out.'

'I'll not say a word,' promised Storm without a qualm. 'I suppose Mr Granville wrote to Harries and –'

'Told him to let the workmen have the run o' the Grange,' said Benjamin, not to be robbed of his story. 'That's the size of it, sir. Love us, but they tell me some days there were twenty or thirty men around the Grange.'

'But they haven't been there for a week?' queried Storm.

'I don't know about that, sir. At first they used to come in and have one now and again, sir, but they haven't been down for six or seven days. I was only saying so to poor old Tom, him liking his drop but not being able to carry it well. He said they'd stopped working for a while, sir.'

'What kind of men were they?' demanded Storm. 'Navvies?'

Mr Cripps was definite.

'Bless me, no, sir! Quite gentlemanly men. Wireless engineers I took 'em to be.'

'Well,' said Storm heartily, 'thanks a lot, Mr Cripps. Give us another tankard of that beer and we'll be going.'

Gentlemanly looking men, he thought. Zoeman's crowd for a fortune! He had little doubt but that the Grange had been Zoeman's headquarters for some time, but that the return of the Granvilles had stopped whatever game he had been up to. But what had they been building?'

With a generosity which still further warmed the heart of Mr Benjamin Cripps he waved away the change from a pound note and with Timothy in close attendance, left the inn. The letter to Sir William Divot had already been sent, and its writing had filled in the time they had been forced to wait for the ten o'clock opening of *The Four Bells*. What the Assistant Secretary would say when he received it Storm hated to think.

Timothy pressed the self-starter of the Bugatti and the great car roared into action.

There was only one possible interpretation, Storm decided, of the 'wireless thingummy' and the horde of workmen. During his master's absence Harries had been making hay while the sun shone, and the story of the wireless installation had been spread round to allay suspicion. The Granville's return, some time earlier than had been expected, had put him thoroughly in the cart. No wonder Mrs Harries had gone away with so little fuss! There was no doubt that she had been 'in the know', as had the two gardeners.

Storm was certain that Benjamin Cripps's description of the workmen tallied with Zoeman's men, and he was equally sure that Zoeman had had nothing to do with the killing of Harries. The mystery of the Grange deepened; Storm cursed himself for having lost trace of Perriman and for letting Mrs Harries go.

But that was nothing to his curse when he reached Ledsholm Grange.

The six members of the company were grouped in the hall, unhappy and worried. Two hammers and a couple of pokers supplied evidence of the tapping process in the search for hidden passages, but operations had been abandoned. No one spoke as they entered.

Grimm, standing by the telephone, broke the strained silence.

'Glad to see you back, Martin. I'm afraid – '

Storm went pale.

'For the love of Mike,' he rapped, 'what is it?'

Grimm gulped.

'Just had a chat with the guv'nor,' he said quietly. 'Letty went out with the mater this morning – and she didn't come back!'

13

THINGS UNKNOWN TO
MARTIN STORM

Letty Granville had found it increasingly difficult to look coldly on the genial, boisterous giant with the twinkling blue-grey eyes. On the afternoon when he had burst into the Park Street house and routed Wenlock she had been very nearly at the end of her tether.

But Martin made one big mistake. He had thought blithely that the friendship which he had struck with young Frank Granville would be a sound plank for him to stand on. In point of fact Letty wished heartily that Storm and Granville had never met each other.

She felt resentful towards Frank for a variety of reasons. It had been one of the most difficult and unpleasant tasks of her life to keep Wenlock, vulgarly speaking, on a piece of string during the voyage from New York to Cherbourg, on her brother's behalf.

Frank had worried her for some time. In America he started to work on financial deals which had at first brought him excitement and triumph but had gradually turned him morose and sullen. She read worse trouble in his face one evening in March when he came quietly into the room. His face was white and haggard, his whole demeanour that of a man perilously near losing all confidence.

Pouring himself a whisky and soda he had grinned mirthlessly.

'Letty – I'm deuced sorry, but I'm afraid we – I mean, I've made a thorough mess of things, old girl. Absolute. We're –' He stumbled over the words and had difficulty in meeting her eyes. 'We're dished. Pretty nearly broke.'

It was like saying that the sea had dried up. Broke. It was impossible! She knew that Frank had taken control of over half-a-million pounds after his father's death.

Broke! He was joking!

But looking at him she saw that he had never been further away from joking in his life. He looked haggard and ill, worried almost to death.

'Is it really as bad as that, Frank? Let's talk it over.'

They talked, and at the end of half-an-hour Letty's lips were set in a grimness which only those who had seen and reckoned on the determined mould of her square chin would have expected.

Granville had caught the up-to-date craze of trying to turn one pound into two. The slump, hitting America so hard, had swallowed up the greater part of the Granville inheritance.

'The only thing left,' Frank said uncomfortably, 'is to lease the Grange. We can't sell it. The agreement won't let us. But we can lease it for a tidy bit and keep going.'

In spite of the fact that they had lived away from England for more than five years, he knew that the thought of giving up the Grange would hit his sister harder than any privation. But it was unavoidable.

'You've already arranged it?' she queried in a tight voice. He nodded.

'To a man called Zoeman – Hesketh Zoeman. He says he wants it for six or twelve months, and that the place is just right for an experimental wireless station that he wants to build.'

'And the price?'

'Five thousand a year. It's not so much as I'd have liked, but it's better than nothing. I've fixed up to stay there for a few days when we go back –'

'Go back?' She looked her surprise. 'But why – '

'We'll have to stay here for a month or two,' he told her unhappily, 'until I see how much we can salvage. But we can't keep travelling in – style – and we can't potter about from country to country forever. We'll have to settle down, and you wouldn't like to get a small place out of England, would you?'

'No,' agreed Letty quietly. 'We'd better go back.'

She was as much concerned over the change in her brother as the loss of money. Frank had seemed to be acting a part with her for a long time, and she still felt uneasy. Was it possible that he had told her only a part of the story?

Two months and more passed before he spoke of the journey again, during which time he collected what little there was left of the fortune. As the date of sailing grew closer she felt more than ever that he was keeping something back.

Then a week before they were due to sail he burst into her room, unnaturally bright-eyed and worried much more than he would admit. His concern had been over a man named Wenlock. Five minutes afterwards she met him.

She found him presentable enough, but she could not repress a dislike of the man's flaunting of his physical perfection, nor the glinting power of his green eyes. He seemed to exert an influence over Frank which amounted to little less than fascination; she could have sworn that the younger man was living in fear of Ralph Wenlock.

When the red-haired man had gone, Frank dropped his next bomb.

'There's just a chance, old girl, that Wenlock'll take over Ledsholm Grange! He'll double Zoeman's price – '

'But Zoeman's got the agreement,' she objected.

'Probably we can get over that,' he persuaded. 'Letty, please keep him interested. You can if you will.'

His anxiety to keep both Zoeman and Wenlock interested and his desperate endeavours to get hold of more money strengthened her fears. It took her two full hours to force the truth out of her brother. When it came it was a thousand times blacker than before.

They not only lacked money, but they owed it. The figure of their commitments staggered her, but the fact that Frank was in imminent danger of prosecution staggered her still more! They had to find a hundred thousand pounds. He reckoned to get what he could from Zoeman, what he could from Wenlock, and take a risk on speculative markets for the other. If it failed –

'Letty' – he was absolutely at the last gasp she knew – 'you'll back me up, won't you? If I thought you wouldn't – '

She said stiffly: 'Of course I'll back you up.'

It wasn't until they had reached Southampton and Wenlock was sulking after the affair with Storm that she realised the dangerous game her brother was playing. A chance remark from Wenlock told her that the fight between him and the unknown Zoeman for Ledsholm Grange turned on crime.

She shrank from taking any action, torn between loyalty to her brother and horror at seeing the frank-faced, blunt-speaking and scrupulously honest youth whom she had thought she knew so well change to a near-criminal. Now he dealt in subterfuge and played on her feelings for help. The uncertainty of the future, and the possibility of Martin Storm being mixed up in the business which centred round Ledsholm Grange, added to her torment.

What was Storm's part? Why had Frank staged that affair on deck? She discovered that Wenlock had seen and for some reason been suspicious of Martin Storm and Roger Grimm the first time the cousins had shown their faces on board.

At exactly half-past ten on the morning following her terrifying experience at Ledsholm Grange and her rescue by Martin Storm, Letty Granville, feeling less harassed than at any time since the first bombshell of the financial disaster, finished an admirable breakfast and smiled easily at the small, bright-faced Lady Alicia Grimm. At that identical moment Martin Storm was entering the village post office at Ledsholm.

Lady Alicia took up a small bundle of letters and with a murmured apology scaled them through quickly. Then her bright eyes twinkled.

'One for you, Miss Granville.'

Letty saw, with a pang of disappointment, that it was from Frank.

Excusing herself she opened it, frowning when she found a rough plan of the underground passages which honeycombed Ledsholm Grange.

The briefly pencilled note with it sent the fears and uncertainties of the past months rushing back to her. The note was damning and yet held a ray of hope which she prayed would materialise.

Dear Letty,

I'm in desperate straits but there's just a chance of getting through.

Give this note to the man you will see in a blue Delage, and do just what he says. There's fifty thousand pounds in it!

Frank.

Letty stared in front of her, thankful for Lady Alicia's rapt attention to her varied correspondence. The possibility of escape from the hell of the threat overhanging her brother was the one bright spot. But what was the plan of the underground passages for? What could possibly bring him fifty thousand pounds? And who would be the man in the blue Delage?

Harassed by fear of Wenlock and uncertain of the danger which might surround the unsuspecting Martin Storm, she was in two minds what course to take, but the realisation that if Frank failed to get the money it would mean his certain imprisonment decided her.

She laughed bitterly to herself. He had gradually made it impossible for her to get out of the net which was spreading round them both.

Damn money! Damn money!

It had turned one of the straightest men crooked, and his defection bit more deeply into her heart than she realised.

The hunched, wizened old man with the horrible green eyes which reminded her of the flaming orbs of Ralph

Wenlock peered at Letty from the back of the blue Delage saloon car.

She saw him as she walked down the stone steps of the Philmore Crescent house with Lady Alicia.

The Delage crawled twenty yards behind them as they walked towards Kensington High Street. Outside an antique shop Lady Alicia stopped to admire a Japanese vase and after a tantalizing hesitation decided to buy it.

Letty felt the eyes of the man in the Delage boring into her.

'I'll wait here, if I may,' she said jerkily.

Lady Alicia nodded.

'I won't be a minute, my dear.'

She had hardly disappeared into the shop before the Delage drew up alongside.

A hoarse voice reached Letty.

'You have it?'

She nodded.

'Good. Get in the car.'

'But – '

'Get in, I say!'

The old man's stare seemed to hypnotise her. Repressing a shiver of revulsion, she stepped in, and the car slid into the stream of traffic.

14

FRANK GRANVILLE DISAPPEARS

Storm felt like hell!

There was nothing he could do, nothing which would help. The sortie of the previous afternoon, the trick which he had won against the devilish plans of Redhead, had been made useless. Letty was gone! Storm took a grip on himself with a mighty effort. He knew that, for him the part which Letty Granville was playing in the mystery of Ledsholm Grange dwarfed all other elements. Once he could get her clear again –

'Granville been told?' he demanded suddenly.

Grimm shook his head.

'No. He went out with Horrobin to hash something up for lunch.'

'I'll tell him,' muttered Storm.

None of the others went with him to the kitchen. None of them had seen Martin Storm so badly hit and they felt instinctively that he was best left alone.

Horrobin, with his sleeves rolled up, ploughing dismally through a vast pile of potatoes, looked round nervously at the sound of footsteps.

'Where's Granville?' jerked Storm.

'He just went outside, sir. Shall I call him?'

'I'll go,' said Storm.

The narrow door leading to the courtyard was open. He passed through and looked round. Granville was not in sight.

'Damnation!' he cursed, going further out and peering into the open door of the power-house and the garage with the same lack of success. 'Where the devil has the fellow gone?'

Which question was echoed not once but a hundred times, for Frank Granville had vanished as completely as his sister from the face of the earth!

Storm deliberated on the wisdom of going to London in an effort to trace Letty, but finally decided that he was likely to do more good by concentrating on finding the secret of Ledsholm Grange. The depression which had furrowed his brow after the ominous telephone message from Sir Joseph lifted, but the happy-go-lucky characteristics of the rugged Martin Storm had gone. His grimness injected the rest of the party.

Playing was over, there would be hell to pay before this affair was finished. The disappearances – three within a couple of hours – created a heavy atmosphere of suspense. Things were moving fast to a climax.

'We can reckon,' said Storm, 'that the main trouble here lies in the kitchen or just outside. Perriman went out of the back door and vanished. Granville did the same, and in both instances Horrors was in earshot but heard nothing. There's a hiding place there, and we're going to find it! Bolt that front door, Tim, and make sure the windows are shuttered. We want no surprise attack.'

Horrobin, still disturbed by the grimness of Storm's manner, had dallied considerably with the potatoes and he saw with some relief that the call for food was likely to be still further delayed.

'Get those hammers,' said Storm to the twins, 'and go over the kitchen inch by inch. Best, you'd better have Righteous with you and poke about the power-house, but for heaven's sake don't damage yourselves! Roger, you and I will dig about these sheds' – he pointed to the four small outhouses and the garage – 'and Dodo will keep a look-out.'

'Kind of patrol, what?'

'You've hit it,' said Storm. 'Keep your eyes wide open and trot from end to end of this accursed house. Don't get out of sight and take the silencer off your gun.'

'It shall be done,' muttered Dodo firmly.

For twenty minutes there was no sound but the tapping of iron on steel, wood or stone. Corners, walls, floors and ceilings suffered the onslaught, but the same unresponsive echo came from all.

Crossing to the third outhouse Storm and Grimm saw Martin Best coming from the emergency exit of the power-house. He had contrived to wipe his face with an oil rag and the black smear running from ear to ear leant him a savage look his normally good-tempered countenance did not possess.

Storm waited with his hand on an iron latch as the lumbering Best bore down on them.

'Anything?' he demanded tersely.

'Dunno, old boy. But there's a patch of cement that looks newish. Care to have a squint?'

Storm was already halfway towards the power-house and a moment later all three men were peering at the flooring. After a moment's hesitation Storm pursed his lips in a soundless whistle.

'Been powdered over to make it look old, eh?'

'Looks like it,' agreed Best grimly.

Storm thought rapidly. On the first place the dusting had been done in a hurry, for he was too keenly aware of the astuteness of his opponents to think that the powdered cement had been used from choice. In the second, there were definite passages under and about the Grange.

But Frank Granville had assured him that there were no passages!

He looked round quickly at Roger Grimm.

'Call the others off the hunt, Roger. And tell the twins to bring a couple of pick-axes; they're in the tool shed.'

The twins responded with commendable speed. Within ten minutes of Grimm's message the cement floor of the power-house rang under the combined assault of two picks heaved by Martin Best and Martin Storm, the strongest members of the company.

The new patch proved easy enough to get through. After the first crust of brittleness the picks bit deep. Over the heads of the watching men hovered a tense air of expectancy.

Discovery?

Storm, stretching upwards after a mighty smash, plied his pick again and the blunt point crashed against something much harder than the cement. There was no mistaking the ring of the contact; it was steel on steel!

'Now we're getting somewhere,' he grunted. 'Best – scrape it, don't dig.'

He acted on his own words, scraping the half-dry cement from the steel sheet uncovered by their efforts. Gradually it took shape, revealing a square bounded by grooved lines, a square which was roughly a yard across.

'Any handle?' demanded Toby Arran, craning forward.

Storm shook his head.

'Doesn't seem to be. Probably works on the sliding system – there's no hinge in sight. But we can get round that
with a bit of patience.'

'How?' demanded Derek Milhowel.

'Burn through it,' said Storm. 'How long will it take you
to get into Lewes, Toby?'

Toby Arran deliberated.

'Twenty minutes,' he said finally.

'You're bound to find an oxy-acetylene outfit somewhere,' mused Storm. 'It'll be safer using one of those than
trying to dig through it or pump holes with our guns. If you
can't borrow one, buy one from a factory. And quick's the
word, old boy.'

Toby Arran swung round to the door.

'Shall I take Tim with me?'

'Better have two of you,' agreed Storm.

He broke off in a sudden fit of coughing, feeling the
tears burn in his eyes as he leaned heavily on his pick.

'Damnation – '

He broke off again, amost doubling up as a second paroxysm of coughing gripped him. Grimm stretched out a
steadying hand, then something bit deep into his throat.
He staggered into Milhowel, choking sickeningly. Milhowel,
sensing the unseen horror which was creeping into the
stuffy little power-house, tried desperately to get to the door,
but before he had taken two steps his body, too, was gripped
in a torturing paralysis starting from a fearful burning at the
back of his throat.

Gas! The realisation struck at them with the icy hand of
death!

Leaning helplessly against the wall the twins coughed
sickeningly, feeling the horror of the ghastly gas which had
been poured into the brick shed. It burned torturingly into

their eyes, rasping their tongues and biting deep into their lungs, constricting them, strangling them, choking them!

Storm, further away from the door than the others, staggered drunkenly from side to side, then dropped in a sagging heap to the floor. Best, his last moment of consciousness filled with the dread of what might happen if any of them touched the live wires, lurched forward and grabbed the control switch. Wildly, desperately, he pressed it down.

Sick with pain, Grimm pointed towards the door which the Arrans tried desperately to reach as they staggered helplessly.

'Tell – the – others!' cracked Grimm. 'Tell – '

With a horrible paroxysm of coughing he crumpled up, striking his head against the thick end of Best's axe.

Timothy Arran reached the door, seeing the blurred figures of Dodo Trale and Righteous Dane rushing towards the power-house. He waved frantically, trying to form words with his scorched lips but muttering only a senseless gabbling. Before they realised the danger Dane and Trale felt the gas biting into them. Too late, they swung round in a mad effort to get out of range.

Through a red mist Trale saw the podgy figure of Horrobin, backing with terror from a man whose dull grey automatic threatened him.

'Zoeman!' gasped Righteous Dane. 'Zoeman!'

He plucked madly at his pocket but before his fingers touched the cold steel of his gun a wave of nauseating sickness swept through his body, sending him lurching to the ground a split-second before Trale, too, collapsed.

Horrobin gave a moan of terror as Zoeman moved towards him. He seemed to feel the lead-nosed bullet tearing through flesh and bone, seemed to feel the horrible warm ooze of his blood –

Then the butt of Zoeman's revolver cracked against his temple, and he dropped like a stone.

The grim-eyed, suave-voiced man in the hall of Ledsholm Grange spoke quickly to the gunman who was pulling on a pair of motoring gauntlets.

'Take Hibbert and Snelling with you, Kurt. Shoot up the whole village if you must, but get that letter!' He swung round to the third man who was standing uneasily at his side. 'If this falls through, Greenaway – '

Greenaway opened his lips in a resentful protest.

'You told me you were busy,' he muttered.

Zoeman cut furiously across his words.

'You crazy fool! Didn't I tell you to report any move from the Grange above everything else? Did you think I was too busy to be told that Storm and the other idiot went into the village – and to the Post Office? Am I dealing with lunatics?'

Greenaway shrank back. Zoeman had never seemed so murderous.

The first man, Kurt, hurried towards the Bugatti which had been left outside the main door by Toby Arran. The Boss was obviously in a rage. Trouble was brewing. He drove ruthlessly over the soft green lawns on his way to the back of the house to pick up reinforcements.

Half-a-dozen men were carrying the inert bodies of Martin Storm and Roger Grimm out of the power-house. A three-yard stretch of the kitchen wall gaped open, showing a flight of rubber-covered stairs leading into the bowels of Ledsholm Grange. The other victims of the gas attack were already below, flung ruthlessly into a room immediately behind the wine-cellar of the great house.

The underground passages which Frank Granville had pooh-poohed to Storm not only existed but, under the direction of Zoeman during the two months in which he had been able to work unhindered, had been fitted up with rubber flooring and two silently moving steel exits worked by the elaborate system of electric control installed immediately beneath the power-house. There were five sizeable rooms as well as that in which Storm's party were sleeping off the effect of the gas.

Zoeman had reckoned on having six months in which to work. The Grange had been leased from Frank Granville and there seemed no fear of discovery. But Granville, bearing warning of the approach of the dreaded American, Redhead, had returned quicker than he had expected, and Martin Storm with his pack of young idiots had caused more trouble than Zoeman would have dreamt possible.

Carefully he had set his plans. From all parts of England members of his organisation had brought off daring robberies, bringing the proceeds to Ledsholm Grange. In the fifth, electrically-controlled room which no-one entered unless he was there himself, the proceeds of the major jewel robberies of the past five months were stored.

But Zoeman's master-stroke was to come, and with the interference of Storm and the threat of Redhead it had been jerked into operation before full maturity, and its success was now jeopardised.

It had taken him longer than he had expected to overcome the resistance of Martin Storm and his band of fools. He had been forced to wait until he had them altogether, to make sure that none of them had a chance to escape. Could he hold out long enough against Redhead? Redhead, the man who made even the crime-steeped blood of American gangsters freeze.

Cool, calculating, clever, Zoeman believed that it was possible. Ledsholm Grange was absolutely isolated, and he reckoned he could stand against an attack from the American.

But Storm had dealt a crushing blow against him. Through the negligence of the man Greenaway, the journey to the village had not been reported. Zoeman, fearing an S O S to the police, sent Kurt and the others to hold-up Ledsholm Post Office and its spinster mistress.

There was a chance of trouble when the hold-up was reported certainly, but hold-ups were everyday affairs up and down the country, most of them connected with Zoeman's organisation. There was no reason why suspicion should fall on the Grange.

Strangely, he felt an unrestricted admiration for Martin Storm.

Who was he? What part was he playing in the police and secret service efforts to get to the root of the bandit outrages which had startled and unnerved the country? Zoeman thought of the department at Whitehall – 'Z' Department – and pursed his lips. He was uneasy about 'Z' Department.

It was just after twelve when the post mistress of the village – one Jane Simms on whom Benjamin Cripps had for some time been casting an interested eye – heard a car drawing up outside the store.

A lean, sharp-featured man stepped quietly into the shop.

She stared with sudden terror at the gun in the man's hand, but her scream died on her lips.

'Half a word,' snapped Kurt, 'and you're for it!'

Helplessly she watched him empty the post box, saw him collect the registered letters, the loose change, and the postal orders.

Kurt worked quickly and effectively.

He wasn't sure what to do with the woman. He was half-afraid that she might have recognised him, for he had been through the village from the Grange several times. But Zoeman had given instructions that there was to be no killing except in extreme emergency. So, killing was out.

Still keeping his gun trained on her, he stepped towards the fear-stricken woman. The scream which sprang to her lips died in a rasping gurgle as he brought the gun crashing on her unprotected head.

Dragging her body behind the counter, he hurried to the waiting Bugatti.

Benjamin Cripps, standing at the door of his hostelry, stared in disappointment at the car as it roared along the dusty road.

'I had hoped,' he said disconsolately, 'that gentlemen 'ud be popping in agen. Mebee Jane knows where he's gone.'

The patriarch to whom he addressed this remark shook his head.

'Jane Simms ne're did like being called in t'shop twix' twelve an' one. Leave it a bit, I say.'

'Aye,' agreed Benjamin, whose eyes had been on Jane since the decent period of mourning after his wife's death had expired. 'Aye, mebee ye're right, gaffer.'

Zoeman saw the returning figure of Kurt with keen relief.

'The letters?'

'Registers and all,' grinned Kurt. 'Want me again?'

'Get below,' ordered Zoeman, 'and close up every entry excepting the chapel one. And keep two men outside Storm's place. They're a good deal smarter than they look.'

Five minutes afterwards he stared stonily down at the twenty opened envelopes.

Storm's letter was not among them!

15

REDHEAD

Three men sat at a small table in the dining room of the house of Mr Sommers Lee-Knight in Park Street, Mayfair. One was Ralph Wenlock, son of the mighty oil magnate who ruled the worldwide organisation of the Wenlock Oil Corporation. His nervous face was twisted and his green eyes smouldered in ill-repressed fury.

'Why the devil didn't you warn me?' he muttered. 'You told me to lease Ledsholm from the Granvilles. I didn't know Zoeman was there.'

The middle man of the three stared at him with a cold, demoniacal expression. Wenlock could never remember the time when he had not been frightened of his calculating, inhuman parent. Since he had arrived in England his fear had grown into overwhelming dread of this hunched, wizened old man whose horrible green eyes – eyes which had hypnotised Letty Granville less than eight hours before – were a thousand times more cruel than his own.

Saul Wenlock had carried out the double role of the worst-feared, most powerful gangster overlord in America and the chief of the Wenlock Oil Corporation for years.

Cursed with a lust for money and power he had exploited both with the cunning of a distorted genius.

He had always carried out his illegal activities under the cloak of another man's personality, and only three of the host of minor barons ruling with fear and being ruled by their legendary overlord with dread, knew Redhead as Saul Wenlock.

Two of them he had shot in cold blood, murdered as they had murdered others on his instructions. They had known too much – what was even more heinous, they had wanted too much. The third was Gazzoni the Italian, the man who had rented the house from Sommers Lee-Knight. Sleek, oily-tongued, swarthy-skinned, he sat with the Wenlocks at the small table.

Gazzoni's finger on the trigger of a gun was quicker than a hawk's swoop on its prey; and Gazzoni's head for figures and diabolical ingenuity was second only to his subservience to Redhead. He was loyal – although treachery was bread and butter in the racketeer's larder – because he knew that Redhead wanted to leave the racket, and that he himself would step into the man's shoes, taking over the power which the fearful influence of the older man had created.

Redhead's European coup was to be his last. His plan of action, swift, murderous, paralysing, would bring a colossal reward!

But for the moment all that mattered in that small room was the struggle between father and son.

Redhead's voice, harsh, guttural and shiveringly cold, cut through the silence.

'I told you to follow the Granvilles to London, and make arrangements for renting Ledsholm Grange. And you didn't even discover that Granville had already let the place to Zoeman! You fool! Did I tell you to kidnap the girl? Did

I tell you to fight? Did I tell you to set Storm and his fools on the alert? You damnable fool! Three months I have been watching Zoeman. I knew that he was at Ledsholm Grange but I didn't know he had rented it. I have been waiting for the moment to strike – and you – '

Ralph Wenlock cowered back as the old man's eyes, blazing with fury, seemed to leap towards him. He was stiff and cold with fear.

'I – I – '

'Be quiet!' hissed Redhead. 'Telephone to the ship and make sure that we are ready for immediate sailing. Collect the men and be in readiness at the garage. If you do a thing without permission – *I'll kill you!*'

The younger man slunk out of the room, too cowed to show fight. Yet he was angry and resentful. Redhead, damn him, meant what he said!

He had known nothing of the state of affairs in England. His father had called him from the United States, telling him to follow the Granvilles and to get possession of Ledsholm Grange. He had also told him to watch out for members of the English Secret Service –

He had heard rumours and had acted on them. Rumour said that Martin Storm and Roger Grimm were members of the dreaded 'Z' Department – and Wenlock had put the great machine of the gangster organisation into action against them.

And he had failed! Both of them had escaped, both of them had laughed him to scorn! They had even avoided injury on the dock at Southampton; and they had brought Redhead's devilish wrath on his head by the defence at Ledsholm Grange.

But for Storm he would have won through. But for Storm he would have gained possession of the Grange, frightened

Granville out of it and sent his report to Redhead with the smirk of success. But for Storm –

All the hatred which the imperturbable Englishman had stirred in him on board the *Hoveric* burst into flame. As he took the wheel of the car standing outside the Park Street house his malevolent fury, his capacity for treachery and vengeance, blazed. Vengeance on Martin Storm, on Zoeman, on the Granvilles –

Treachery to Redhead!

But he followed his instructions. The ship which was waiting in readiness for the getaway of Redhead and his gangsters when the master coup – the attack on Zoeman and the seizure of the vast store of stolen money and jewels secreted at Ledsholm Grange – was completed, was on the alert.

He had telephoned to Plymouth from a garage on the Great West Road just outside Chiswick. The *Utopia Garage* was the last word in up-to-date equipment and luxury. It was owned, according to the registered particulars at Somerset House, by a group of Americans, and on the list of names could be read that of Saul Wenlock, President of the Wenlock Oil Corporation.

Of necessity there were a great number of engineers and garage hands there day and night, and for the greater comfort of his staff Mr Wenlock had built a special wing to the garage in which they could eat, sleep, amuse themselves and reflect on the generosity of their employers.

Those members of the staff who came into direct contact with the general public were English; those who kept in the background were American – and tough Americans. It was not generally known that ten of the hire cars were never let out on hire, nor that they had super-charged engines and that their structure was reinforced with bullet-proof steel.

But that part of the business was kept under Saul Wenlock's hat.

The plan was simple. On the chosen day and at the chosen hour the signal would go forth. The ten cars would set out on supposedly innocent jobs and converge on Ledsholm Grange. Zoeman would be attacked, his vast store of illgotten wealth would be removed to the cars, and the homeward journey would commence; but not to London.

Just outside Plymouth Sound the *Florida Moon,* Saul Wenlock's luxury yacht, was waiting with the ostensible purpose of giving employees of the English company a sea voyage. The happy employees would arrive at the port and embark with the morning tide. Actually the 'employees' would be the gangsters, and their suitcases would contain not clothes but valuables.

It was a clever scheme and there was no reason why it should fail, although the need for quick action – due to the interference of Storm and his men – certainly created an element of risk which would have been eliminated if the plans had been allowed to mature slowly. Redhead, however, was confident of success; callous, inhuman, utterly ruthless, he had seen the advantage of the isolation of Ledsholm Grange. It would be hours before the attack was discovered by the authorities – and there was the possibility that Zoeman, in fear of the police, would exert every effort to keep it secret.

Ralph Wenlock gave the 'get ready' signal to the garage hands and went into consultation with three rough-neck members of the inside staff. He went back to his own car, and an hour later the three gangsters slipped away from the garage. Treachery and vengeance were in the air.

❧ ❧ ❧

Redhead watched his son disappear through the door of the small dining-room.

His quick mind was working tortuously and ruthlessly towards his objective. He knew, through those channels which cover the underworld as thoroughly as Reuter covers the globe, what plans Zoeman had made and how he was working towards his getaway.

Rumours and confirmation had reached America of the bandit organisation which was sending the usually imperturbable Scotland Yard into a frenzy of excitement. Redhead knew that the amount of the hauls must total close on ten million pounds – or nearly thirty million American dollars! The lure was tremendous and the chances of he himself snatching it from under Zoeman's nose, great.

Redhead knew, as he sat at that table, that Zoeman would be preparing for his last effort and escape, and he set his smoothly working machinery into action. Gazzoni's little eyes were fixed on him as he moved towards a cupboard and took out a bottle of whisky and two glasses. He poured out a generous measure of neat spirit, then motioning Gazzoni to pour out his own liquor, tossed his head back, and swallowed it at a gulp.

His voice came startlingly: 'We'll do it tonight, Gazzoni. Is everything ready?'

The dago's sleek head nodded.

'Everything. 'Cepting – if yer kid don't git fly agen.'

'He doesn't know the girl's here again, does he?'

'Nope. But he don't like being bawled out an' I'm wond'ring – '

He stopped, seeing an expression in Redhead's eyes which spelt 'warning'.

'Say, Boss! I didn't mean nuthin'!'

Redhead's hands, gripping the back of a chair with brutal force, jerked upwards suddenly and the chair crashed against the wall four yards away.

'So! You don't mean nulhin', Gazzoni? Well, I'll say you meant a lot! Reckon the kid's likely to double-cross, eh?'

'Say!' Gazzoni's little eyes narrowed. 'I wouldn't say that, Boss. You got me all wrong – '

'Quit lying, Gazzoni! You reckon he'll make a break on his own. And by God, I'm not so sure you're wrong. That's why I sent him out. He'll be through in half-an-hour and then we'll see. Where's that plan?'

Gazzoni pulled a leather case from his pocket. The small scale plan of the underground passages at Ledsholm Grange was slipped on to the table.

Redhead peered intently. He knew the plan by heart, but there were several points to square up before he finished.

'The girl reckons you can get in by the wine-cellar, doesn't she?'

Gazzoni nodded. He had spent half-an-hour with Letty Granville, and the threat of his cruel hands had sent fear into her heart.

'She sure does, Boss. Zoeman's been working at the back – that's what the brother told you, ain't it?'

Redhead nodded. His one interview with Frank Granville had been fruitful, and with the plan was well worth the big money that he had paid.

'Meaning,' rasped Gazzoni, 'that he's left the front of the place alone, using the dungeons for hiding in and keeping the sparklers. See that line there –?'

He pointed at the line showing the wall between the wine cellar and the first of Zoeman's rebuilt vaults.

'The girl says that there used to be a door joining the wine cellar to the other dungeons. But it was bricked up when she and her brother were kids. But you see what I mean, Boss? Just a stick or two of powder and the wall's blown down. We're right through before Zoeman knows it.'

'Hump. Well – twenty men will be enough. We'll send the rest down to Plymouth to get on the ship right away. You've got the hired hands for the garage?'

'All ready,' Gazzoni assured him. To make sure that no comment was caused by a heavy decrease in staff at the *Utopia Garage,* three dozen new workmen had been engaged, recruited from the sweepings of London. If any query was raised the others had gone on the Wenlock Corporation President's cruise for his employees.

Redhead's green eyes flared. Knowing nothing of Zoeman's gas attack he thought that Storm and his men were still occupying the front of the Grange, and his hatred for the band of hectic young Englishmen had been simmering since their first interference.

'We'll get inside the front hall if we have to blow it down, Gazzoni! When we're through the cellar cut for the stuff and get it in the cars. Have two men at the back and two at the front so that we can get out both ways.' He refilled his glass with neat whisky. 'Don't play with Storm. I want them dead!'

'Reckon Zoeman's got thirty million dollars there,' muttered Gazzoni avariciously. 'All in one kick and it ain't cost us more'n a hundred thousand to do it! Some job, I'll say!'

'Some job all right, Gazzoni. But it's not finished yet. Check up on that telephone and see what the kid's done.'

He was relieved five minutes later to hear that the younger man had followed his instructions to the letter. The possibility of his son double-crossing him had made him hesitate. The job had to be done in one ruthless swoop. Before a whisper of the attack reached the authorities the gangsters had to be on board the *Florida Moon,* and an hour lost through treachery might prove fatal.

Taking the telephone from Gazzoni he rasped final instructions to the 'manager' of *Utopia Garage.* After an interval he was repeating his orders to the waiting men on the *Florida Moon,* through agents at a local hotel.

Large motor launches were waiting in readiness to take the gangsters to the yacht. If there were rumours after this last staggering coup it mattered less than nothing. The *Florida Moon* was going to founder on the first day out!

The plans were perfect. The ship had been carefully rigged by his own men so that within two hours it would change from a luxury yacht to a third-class South American liner which was registered at Lloyds. The liner would receive one despairing message from the *Florida Moon.*

S O S. Sinking fast. S O S.

And thereafter there would be silence. No-one would ever hear of Wenlock or his employees. No-one would know that a certain South American country was sheltering him, no-one would know that all his vast resources had been turned into cash and utilised in the establishment of his own little community, peopled by his men and prepared carefully and slowly for years in readiness for his getaway.

The world could know that Redhead was Saul Wenlock. For the world would think that he had been swept into oblivion, swallowed by the deep waters of the ocean.

Yes – his plans were perfect!

With the element of risk reduced to the absolute minimum, he felt that complacency which was his only weak spot. All that mattered now was the one mighty swoop at Ledsholm Grange.

He reckoned that the attack would take an hour. Timing his blow for three o'clock he could cut across country and be at Plymouth by half-past four at the latest. The *Florida Moon* would be on its way to oblivion by five o'clock.

It was colossal! It was perfect!

Redhead's features were twisted into a gloating grin of complacent satisfaction. Gazzoni looked into his glowing green eyes and saw the animal ferocity in them.

'Right,' rasped Redhead. 'Now – it's nearly five. Better phone Fortnums for some dinner. Dinner for three at half-past six. No – make it six.'

Gazzoni's foxy face showed his surprise.

'Three, Boss?'

'Three!' rasped Redhead. 'We're having company, Gazzoni. The girl. Reckon she's earned it, eh?'

Grudgingly Gazzoni lifted the telephone again, and gave the order.

'Fetch her,' Redhead ordered suddenly.

Gazzoni made his way up the narrow stairs on which Storm and the twins had been surprised by Ralph Wenlock on the previous evening, while downstairs Redhead congratulated himself on the astuteness of his move with the girl. Of course, he couldn't have worked it without Granville and the fifty thousand pounds that he had paid for the plans. It was a lot of money, but he had preferred to pay it into Granville's bank rather than chance a squeal to the police from the owner of Ledsholm Grange.

But he agreed with Gazzoni. The girl was dangerous. She would have to be got rid of.

16

SHOCKS FOR MARTIN STORM

Pain danced behind Martin Storm's feverish eyes. It jigged a tango across his forehead. He tried to stretch out his hand. A shock ran through him as he discovered that his arm wouldn't move, that something bound his wrists together in front of him. His ankles, when called on, refused to function by the same token.

The overpowering, horrific realisation flashed through his mind that he was tied hand and foot. The aching, throbbing, sawing madness in his head faded as the full force of the devastating knowledge struck home.

Bound hand and foot! Helpless!

Rolling over on his side to ease the rush of blood which had made him dizzy after his efforts to move, he thought back. Slowly but with startling clarity he recalled the investigation at the back of the Grange, the energy with which they had wielded pick-axes on the patch of new cement. He could almost see the bright steel of the concealed door and feel the exhilaration surging through him at the discovery.

Then he remembered the muzziness which had filled his head, the awful paroxysm of coughing which had shaken

him from head to foot. He remembered the struggling figures of the others; Grimm, reeling from side to side, his face
set with pain-wracked distortions of grotesque frightfulness.

There was no need to think much further. Whether
Zoeman or Wenlock had been the agent of it, it had been a
gas attack; thank God it had not proved fatal.

He swore coldbloodedly, gripped with fury at the ease
with which he had fallen into the enemy's hands.

'Who the blazing hell is that?' demanded Righteous
Dane thickly. 'What blankety use do you think that blankety
outburst is likely to do, you blankety – '

'It's me,' informed Storm mildly.

'You, is it?' grunted Righteous. Then a new expression
crept into his voice, giving it a sharp edge of new-born hope.
'Are you free, Windy?'

'The answer is no,' murmured Martin. 'However –'

Cursing the blackness and sending lightly winged but
heavy hearted badinage across the intervening yards of gloom
he worked with methodical thoroughness at the cords which
bit deeply into the flesh at his wrists. Dane followed suit.

'None of the others have come round,' murmured
Storm after several minutes. 'Hope they haven't got it too
badly,'

'No need to worry,' said Dane optimistically. 'I reckon
you got the biggest dose, old boy. God! You did look a mess!'

Storm snorted.

'I felt it. Wonder whether Wenlock or Zoeman was
responsible?'

'Zoeman,' answered Dane with certainty. 'Hallo – '

Someone stirred.

'Where the hell – '

'Best old boy,' said Storm, 'think back a bit. Power-house
– Ledsholm Grange – pick-axes – '

149

'Got it!' burst out Best in a hoarse whisper. 'Oh, my – '

'We don't know where we are,' broke in Storm, 'but we think that Zoeman's the villain. It was gloves off, all right,' he conceded. 'But we're bound hand and foot and we can't get away. Do your bit, son.'

There was complete silence from the corner of the room in which Best sat. Storm, straining his eyes as much as he could, managed to distinguish the vague outlines of a body next to him, but only the white blur of the face was visible out of the darkness. Whoever it was was groaning in his enforced sleep, which suggested that he would soon be more lively.

'Creepy kind of shanty,' muttered Storm. 'I reckon we must be underneath the Grange, boys. Here! What's that?'

His query was directed at the invisible Best, who had muttered something fierce but unprintable.

'Of all the blazing furies!' stormed Best. 'I managed to get my pocket knife open, Windy, and the darned thing's gone half-an-inch into m'innards!'

Storm kept silent for a moment which might have been sympathy but was actually in thought. Then:

'Righteous – you're not so heavy as I am. Try and wriggle towards Best. We can do with that knife.'

After five minutes that seemed a year Dane's voice, soft but triumphant, signalled the fact that he had reached the still suffering Best. Moving with extreme care he got a grip of the blade, drew it out of Best's pocket and set to work sawing through the cords tying the big man's wrists.

'Lumme, but it's tough!' he muttered.

'Do leave me a *bit* of flesh on me bones, old boy. Ah! That's it! Give me a minute to make my wrists work and I'll do the same for you.'

It was exactly ten minutes by the hands of Best's illuminated watch when Roger Grimm, still only partly awake and the last of the party to regain consciousness, was freed. The wound in his cheek from the edge of the axe felt stiff but had not reached the bone. The others were standing about conversing in tense whispers, easing their cramped limbs.

'Shh!' snapped Storm suddenly.

A silence of the dead settled over the room as his voice faded. Footsteps could be heard.

By a process of linking hands and creeping steadily round the walls, the imprisoned men located the door. There were no windows, thus giving colour to the belief that they were below Ledsholm Grange. Next to the door was a lighting switch which worked. Storm turned the brilliant white glow out as soon as they had taken a brief look round the bare walls of the empty vault.

For a moment he was half-afraid that the light had been noticed, but a voice from outside reassured him.

'Reckon they're still asleep,' said one man – the unfortunate Greenaway who had failed to report the sortie into the village. 'Think we'd better look in, Browning?'

The second man's voice came cryptically.

'He told us to, didn't he?'

Scarcely daring to breathe the seven prisoners heard the key inserted in the lock. Taking position with a soft-footed caution, Storm made sure that when the door opened he would be able to reach his man in the first second.

On tenterhooks they heard the key turn and a brief rattle as the handle was twisted.

A dazzling beam of light shot into the gloom of the vault as the door opened, revealing the bare patch of floor where there should have been men! Greenaway, holding the light, jumped back as something rammed towards him, but Storm's clenched fist caught him on the point of the jaw, sending his man down in a senseless heap. The torch dropped to the floor and for the first time Zoeman's precaution of lining the walls and floors with rubber reacted adversely for him. Instead of clattering there was only a dull thud.

Storm's free hand shot out suddenly. Before the startled Browning realised what was happening the shout of warning in his throat died with a rasping gurgle. Staggering back he took the quick-footed Timothy Arran's pile-driver in the middle of his stomach. With a sickening ouch! he doubled up.

Stooping down Storm dragged him into the room which was fast emptying of the members of Storm's party. Grimm helped to shift the first man and Dodo picked up the torch.

'Get back inside a minute,' said Storm urgently. 'Hurry, men! Now show a light, Dodo.'

Muttering instructions Storm began to tie short ends of cord together, and within three minutes both of Zoeman's underlings were bound hand and foot.

'Take their keys,' grunted Storm. 'Got 'em, Best? Good man. Anything else?'

Best, with a grin, revealed a brace of automatics.

'Now we're moving. Out in the passage, all of you, and lock the door.'

In single file the seven moved cautiously along the narrow passage in the direction from which the ill-fated guards had come. In the lead, Storm came to the first step of a staircase.

'Two of you stay here,' he muttered, 'in case anyone comes from behind. Keep one of the guns and give a shout if there's any trouble.'

Leaving the reluctant twins behind them the remainder of the party pushed cautiously on.

'Corner here,' Storm muttered. 'Righteous, keep here with Dodo. You'll have to do without a gun, though.'

'What're fists for?' demanded Righteous grandly.

'Stout fellow! Three shouts if you're in trouble, so that we'll know where to go. And don't move singly whatever happens.'

Five yards along the passage Storm, with Grimm and Best close behind him, stopped dead.

Ahead of him, round another sharp bend, a narrow pencil of light showed the outline of a partly open door.

'Quiet, boys,' murmured Storm. He took a firmer grip on his gun and stepped forward.

Outside the door he crouched low, straining his ears for the slightest sound. For a full minute all three men waited with a tense expectancy, their ears cocked for the lowest whisper.

But none came. The room ahead was silent.

'We'll take a chance,' muttered Storm. 'Roger, hold the gun. I'll go in first, on my hands and knees. If there's anyone inside pot 'em without asking questions. Ready?'

'All set,' whispered Grimm, touching the trigger.

Silent as a mouse, Storm crept through the door. No one was there. A glance sufficed to tell him that the room was in general use by a large number of men, and he frowned as he wondered where they were.

Overcoats and an assortment of masculine oddments were scattered about, while on each of five baize-topped tables were packs of cards, some newly dealt and others thrown down in obvious haste in the middle of a game. It was easy to see that there had been an urgent call to action.

Storm pressed out a half-smoked cigarette thoughtfully. At most it had been left five minutes before.

He looked about him.

Straight ahead of them was a second door, securely fastened this time but showing a crack of light.

Storm put his eye to the keyhole. Muttering imprecations on the designer of the lock, he squinted upwards, downwards, left and right in an unavailing effort to see something more helpful than the leg of a table and the toe-cap of an unpolished shoe.

Straining his ears to the utmost he heard a soft, at first unintelligible mutter of voices.

He could not hear the words clearly, but the voice, suave, cool, confident and faintly derisive, was unmistakable; it was the voice of Zoeman.

Storm's lips set in a grim line.

The second voice came more clearly. Not only did he recognise it, he heard the damning words.

'I've got to have the money quickly, Zoeman. I kept a watch on Wenlock and sent messages through to you when it might have meant a bullet in my back at any minute. I've done my share – now I want the money!'

It was the voice of Frank Granville!

17

ESCAPADES AND DISASTERS

Storm knew that he was in love with Letty Granville. It might prove to be dangerous or unwise, but the fact remained and he was glad of it. It would not be the first time in history that such a complication had arisen.

He could now have no doubt of Frank Granville's part in the affair of Redhead. It had occurred to him before that if her brother was playing a double game and fell foul of the police, it would hit Letty harder than the man himself. In consequence he had lulled his fears, but now, hearing those damning words coming through the door he could doubt no longer.

Double-crossing, they called it. Even rogues black-balled a squealer.

Zoeman's voice came again, slightly louder.

'You'll get your money as soon as we've finished.'

'I've done all I promised to do.'

'You didn't get Storm away from the Grange. *And you called him here!*'

Granville laughed harshly.

'You've got a lot to learn about Storm. I daren't let him think that I wanted him to clear out – '

'But,' repeated Zoeman, 'you brought him here.'

'I know I did. Damn it, Zoeman, I'm in the devil of a hole and I've got to get the money. I don't care how. But you were here when Wenlock kidnapped my sister. I wanted to make quite sure that she was safe – '

'Conscience pricking you?' sneered Zoeman.

Granville was silent. None knew better than he the danger into which he had drawn Letty, and it was the one point in his treacherous activities between Zoeman and Wenlock, the constant pitting of one man against the other, selling knowledge earned from one man to the next, which made him uneasy.

Zoeman went on quietly and Storm had difficulty in catching the words.

'All right. We'll let that go. But what was the letter Storm sent off this morning?'

There was uncertainty in his voice and Storm felt a lilt of relief. The letter had gone through. But he set his teeth as Granville gave the information without a pause.

'He wrote to the Home Office – Sir William Divot. He didn't say much, apart from reporting the murder of Harries and the death of Smithers.'

'Smithers killed himself,' said Zoeman. 'He was too yellow to take what might come. Harries – that was Wenlock's work, blast him!' There was a pause, then: 'So he wrote to Divot, did he? God! We'll have to move!'

There was a scraping of chairs, and for a moment Storm thought the men were coming to the door; but the shuffling stopped suddenly.

'He didn't take it anywhere else but Ledsholm, did he?'

'No. He must have caught the special morning post at ten-forty-five. A train only stops at Ledsholm Halt on market days.'

Zoeman's voice was steely.

'We'll be lucky if we get out of this alive. I can't leave yet. There are a dozen more men to come in before ten o'clock. Are you standing by? Or clearing out?' There was a wealth of contempt in the words.

'I'll stay,' muttered Granville.

He's got guts, thought Storm, the courage of utter desperation.

'I'm sending you down to the village,' said Zoeman smoothly, 'with two men. If you try any tricks you'll get shot without a thought. Tell the man Cripps that you're having a film company at Ledsholm Grange this evening, and that there might be a war scene taken. That,' he added slowly, 'is in case Redhead comes. We should have to fight. Anyhow – make sure that the whole village knows about it, and stress the possibility of danger. Tell Cripps that you will prosecute anyone trespassing on the grounds of the Grange. Got that?'

'There are two public roads running through,' said Granville.

'We'll have to chance that. And don't forget that if we don't get away with it tonight you'll lose your money. You'll go down in the Bugatti, and it shouldn't take more than an hour.'

Storm heard Granville's footsteps crossing the room and a door open and close. Mixed with rage at the treachery of Granville was a deep respect for the cleverness of Zoeman. That story of a film shooting was little short of genius. It would disarm local suspicion if there was any shooting, and no rumours would spread round to the authorities. What was more, as many cars as Zoeman wanted could go to and fro.

He was fairly sure of the position of affairs. Zoeman had sent his men out on a country-wide series of hold-ups and robberies. He would not desert his men, yet the leader of the English bandit organisation was on tenterhooks, deadly afraid of that letter to Sir William Divot.

But Storm's fury towards Granville was strong and deep. Out of his own mouth he had been convicted of double-crossing from the start. Even on board the *Hoveric* he had known that Zoeman was at the Grange – and he remembered that Granville had been in consultation with Ralph Wenlock. Was he planning to sell out to both sides?

And how much did Letty know?

Swinging round to his two followers, he whispered tersely:

'Granville's ratted. Zoeman's in there alone. If the door's unlocked we'll get him. If it's not, we'll wait until he goes and see what we can do with the keys.'

The others nodded grimly, feeling something of Storm's fury at the treachery of Frank Granville. Scarcely daring to breathe, Storm put his fingers on the brass handle of the door and turned it gently.

A glint of satisfaction brightened the grimness of his eyes at the ease with which it was done. Motioning Grimm with his left arm he waited until that worthy was standing so that his gun was in position to cover the gang leader. Then:

'Now!' he muttered.

The door crashed open. Zoeman jerked to his feet in a trice, but the gun in Grimm's hand spoke louder than words and he kept his hands away from his pockets. The expression on his usually suave features was not pleasant.

Storm stepped quickly to the further door and turned the key. Slipping it in his pocket he swung round.

'So,' he murmured.

Zoeman made a tremendous effort to regain his self-control. After that first moment of icy fury his features had relaxed. He stared coolly at the genial giant in front of him, not flinching as Storm took two steps towards him and gently slid his automatic from his hip pocket.

'I'd hate to crack you one, Zoeman. Funny, isn't it, the way things go? An hour ago you wouldn't have believed this could happen.'

Zoeman swallowed.

'I certainly wouldn't,' he admitted suavely. 'You're the most troublesome pest I've ever come across, Storm. How did you manage it?'

'Trade secret,' said Storm blandly. 'You see us gassed, but workable.'

'You asked for the gas,' Zoeman said smoothly. 'You had chances enough to get away. But' – he smiled mockingly, and the smile gave Storm a qualm. Zoeman looked much less like a man who had been outwitted than he should have done – 'as for the guards – you can take it from me, the rest of my little party won't be too long.'

'Just what we're hoping,' grinned Storm. 'The boys are spoiling to knock somebody's head off.'

Zoeman leaned across the table, and his fingers played with what looked to Storm like a knot in the wood. The expression in his eyes was half-cynical, half-derisive.

'Is that so? Well – let me be explicit, Storm. A large number of my men are upstairs, keeping a look-out. They are watching a signal board set in the wall, and at a certain warning they will know that there is danger down here – '

'Good,' said Storm, 'but not good enough. I'm past the stage when bluff can get over me.'

The smaller man smiled mockingly.

'Seeing should be believing. You may have noticed that all the doors are made of steel. They are electrically controlled. If you look round you will see that the door through which you came and which you left open is now shut.'

Storm was ready for a trap.

'Have a look at it, Roger,' he said sharply.

Grimm turned his head.

Zoeman was speaking the truth. The door was shut behind them.

'So,' murmured Zoeman, 'unless it is opened from the outside it will stay shut – and every other door in the place as well!'

Storm swallowed. Like Best and Grimm he knew that Zoeman was not bluffing. They were trapped almost as certainly as if they had never escaped from their first prison.

'Awkward, isn't it?' murmured Zoeman.

'Deucedly,' managed Storm, breaking through the coldness which had gripped him and forcing a breezy simulation of indifference. 'The trouble is that you are here with us.'

'That won't help you. If anything should happen to me you would still be locked in. So would the other men outside this room. And unless they are extremely careful they will touch one of the doors incomplete ignorance. And the result would be extremely unpleasant.'

'So you say.'

'So you will too – if you're alive to say it,' said Zoeman with a dry smile. 'You may remember that the unfortunate Smithers killed himself by electrocution. *Every door in this place is alive with a current strong enough to kill a man at the slightest touch!*'

Storm stared at him aghast. Suddenly, awfully, he caught a mental vision of the distorted, pain-wracked face of the under-gardener.

'You – swine!' he swore. 'I'll break every bone in your body!'

'Heroics,' mocked Zoeman. 'I merely took precautions against men like Wenlock. You are unfortunate – and I warned you often enough to get out. Meanwhile your friends are in very grave danger.'

Storm made a last desperate effort to beat the other man's resource.

'You're bluffing, damn you!'

With a chilling indifference to the threat of Grimm's automatic Zoeman stood up easily.

'Watch,' he said.

A housefly was circling the room, then straight as a die it sped towards the steel. A prick of blue flame shot out. Storm watched, fascinated, as minute specks of charred powder wafted lazily to the floor.

'I think,' murmured Zoeman, 'that I'd better have the guns, Storm. Otherwise – '

It was the first time in his thirty exuberant years that Martin Storm handed over his weapons without a fight. The cleft stick into which Zoeman had forced him by the remorseless perfection of every detail of his plans threatened a disaster too horrible to countenance.

'Let him have yours, Roger,' he muttered to Grimm. 'No use asking for it. It's another trick to him.'

A gleam of admiration shone in Zoeman's eyes. He could realise without effort the galling madness of Storm's heart as he struck his flag.

'The last trick,' said Zoeman meaningly.

'Maybe not,' grinned Storm. 'Very sound postal service we've got, Zoeman – especially on market days!'

The other's steely grey eyes glinted.

'There was,' he said suavely, 'an unreported raid on the post office this morning, Storm. But we must think of your friends.'

He moved slowly towards the table and pressed another seeming knot in the wood. Once – twice – thrice. A distant buzzer hummed out, and after a short pause there came a tap on the outer door.

'Come in,' said Zoeman, 'but be careful. Our friends here are – '

'Zoeman,' said Storm suddenly and with obvious annoyance, 'I like you – at times. But I should hate to be friends. Nevertheless – '

He was smiling, but there was a hard glint in his blue eyes, striking Zoeman as the sign of a sternly repressed fury, but telling Roger Grimm and Martin Best that he had been seized with an idea. Storm's ideas were usually hairbrained and always risky, but any one of them would be better than complete surrender. They watched him as he strode towards the mocking Zoeman and the three armed men stepping into the room.

'You're talking too much,' said Zoeman, but his eyes narrowed as Storm, standing immediately below the electric lamp stretched his arms upwards. Then:

'Damnation!' he rapped. 'Get him!'

For Storm, with a well-feigned yawn, heaved his great body upwards and in the last split-second of light his fingers gripped the bulb of the lamp. Zoeman's finger touched the trigger of his gun as the frail glass smashed. Three yellow stabs of light spat through the sudden, all-pervading darkness, and three ominous zutts! told the tale of humming bullets. Zoeman heard a heavy fall in front of him and a short, repressed gasp of pain. Storm was hit!

'Crowd the door!' shouted Zoeman, disturbed out of his usual calm. 'Don't fire!'

Best and Grimm heard the order and realised that Storm had foreseen it. In the darkness Zoeman dared not let his men shoot for fear of getting in the path of a death-dealing bullet. They knew, too, that Storm, no matter how badly injured, would have cursed if he thought they hesitated. Tightening their muscles they hurtled like rockets towards the three men at the door. Three white blurs of the men's faces loomed out of the darkness. Best, a yard ahead of Grimm, crashed out his right fist and took his man amidships. The man went down with a cry of agony.

'One!' snapped Grimm, and let fly with his left.

He felt a man's head jerk back with a sickening crack. Taken full on the point of the jaw with every ounce of fury-inspired strength Zoeman's second henchman gasped one rattling gurgle and dropped back.

'Two!' growled Best. 'No you don't, drat you!'

The third man swung round, racing madly for the door, but Best's six-feet-three of bone and muscle catapulted through the air in a flying tackle. The third gunman felt his shins grabbed and he went jerking upwards, crashing his head against the ceiling. Best dodged aside, hearing the dull thud of the senseless body hitting the rubber-covered floor.

'Three,' grunted Best. 'Here's the door, Grimm. Turn right, old son.'

They could see nothing behind them but from the frantic buzzing of the electric bell ahead knew that Zoeman was pressing his warning buzzer. Somewhere ahead they heard a shout of alarm. They waited, crouching like tigers. A flood of light surged through the darkness but undaunted they leapt blindly into the small crowd of gunmen crushing towards Zoeman's room.

Right and left they smashed out grimly, meeting flesh and bone with sickening force. Devastated by that bull rush the crowd split in two. A man's heavily shod foot cracked against Best's shin and with an elephantine bellow the infuriated Best let drive with his right foot. Someone shrieked and a loaded automatic dropped to the floor from nerveless fingers. In a flash Grimm was on it. Pushing ferociously ahead with Best a yard behind him, he fired point-blank beneath his arm at the shattered crowd.

Once – twice – thrice –

'What about Windy?' gasped Best. 'Had we better – '

Before he finished Storm's voice burst furiously.

'Get out, you lunatics! I'm all right!'

Like men possessed they rushed onwards. A fourth empty room still littered with the remains of a meal led to a short flight of stairs, and again Zoeman's precaution of making his underground headquarters soundproof reacted adversely for him. Two gunmen keeping guard over the open steel door leading to the kitchen knew nothing of the second outbreak until a bullet from Grimm's gun sent one man down and Best's great fist hurtled the second against the wall.

It was still daylight. Two men at the door of the powerhouse saw them and their hands darted towards their hip pockets, but the fifth shot from Grimm's automatic took one in the chest, sending him staggering back. With lightning fury Best's fist crashed his companion to the earth.

'Only one more bullet,' muttered Grimm. 'If only we had a car! Tarnation, Best! The Bugatti!'

Timothy Arran's racing monster was standing idly in the courtyard. In less than a second Grimm had swung into the driver's seat, pressing the self-starter and stepping on the gas as Best clambered after him. The great car leapt forward.

From left and right bullets winged towards them, cracking ominously against the bodywork. Half-a-dozen of Zoeman's gang of plunderers, guarding the Grange from concealed points of vantage, kept up a rattling hail of shots, but the Bugatti bore a charmed life. Neither the engine nor the tyres were touched as it swung on two wheels round the gateway of the drive, shaving Black Rock and heading for Ledsholm.

'We're away, boys!' gasped Grimm, madly exultant.

Neither of them saw the Delage with its red-haired driver until it was too late. Then with a startled oath Grimm recognised the green-eyed Wenlock. Before Grimm realised the danger Wenlock pulled at his brakes, barking a word of command to the three gangsters with him.

Jerking out of their seats they dropped out of the car a fraction of a second behind Wenlock who, recognising the Bugatti and the battle-scarred occupants, pressed hard on his accelerator before jumping cleanly into the road.

Grimm fought like a demon to save the Bugatti, but the powerful Delage was too near. Twenty yards away Best accepted the inevitable.

'Jump for it!' he bellowed. 'Out, Roger!'

Something seared redhot through his shoulder as he jumped for the road. He crashed downwards. Grimm, a split-second behind, dodged Wenlock's first bullet but grunted with pain as a second thudded into his thigh. His gun went flying over the hedge as Wenlock leered triumphantly towards his victims a fraction of a second before the two cars crashed with a terrific roar.

'Not quite the last trick,' murmured Martin Storm, looking affably into the glinting grey eyes of Zoeman.

Zoeman's lips curled.

'What about a spot of lint and a bandage?' Storm went on cheerfully. 'Mind you,' he added waggishly, 'a couple of inches more and I'd have been dead. And that's murder, little man!'

Beneath the bright light of a new bulb Zoeman's lined face showed up haggard and worn. The strain of the last twenty-four hours culminating in the escape of Best and Grimm was telling even on his iron nerve. The first half-dozen of his men had returned from their escapades but the main army was still to come. Thirty men had been sent out, travelling in threes and driving super-charged cars.

He knew that the telephone wires of a hundred police stations were buzzing furiously. Attack after attack had been made on banks and post offices. Money, jewels and negotiable bonds had run in a never ceasing and ever increasing stream into the hands of his armed bandits in this last final coup. It was the biggest, most complete and most successful outburst of perfectly organised crime that had ever been attempted.

Zoeman reckoned that at least two million or more pounds would be added to the millions that he had stored at Ledsholm Grange! Two million pounds in one great swoop in defiance of the police!

And not one of the bandit cars had been held up!

Nevertheless the slightest leakages of information would bring an army of police to the Grange. Grimm and Best had escaped, and even the twelve hours' grace to be counted on before Storm's letter would reach London had been snatched away! There was nothing to do but clear out with the colossal fortune already packed in small cases and ready for immediate handling when his men returned. The packages had been prepared during the past hour, and his call to action had caused the desertion of the rooms through which Storm and the others had passed. But he couldn't move before they returned.

Zoeman had turned to crime after a life of careful effort to secure a position worth having in the business world. After four years of hell in Flanders, he discovered that the biggest sin in the eyes of the world is lack of money. For a long time he had played with the idea of crime but the element of risk and the odds against success stopped him.

As a branch manager of the English section of the Wenlock Oil Company he had an opportunity for a visit to America, and discovered accidently the identity of Redhead. It determined him. Steadily he formed his plans, building up an organisation of young, iron-nerved men, lawless, anti-social.

The idea of pooling the resources of the various hold-ups and storing all but that needed for immediate operations gave each man of his company of criminals something to work for and a granite reason for loyalty. Gradually he worked towards his great finale, a countrywide series of robberies, return to Ledsholm Grange and getaway. He was wise enough to realise that the longer the activities of his gang were drawn out the greater the chance of discovery and capture.

He was ready for the emergency when it came. Redhead and Storm had discovered his identity and knew his headquarters. He would have preferred more time, but on the morning of the gas attack his fleet of cars set out on the errands of pillage, still given the definite order of 'no killing'.

But the recent developments had put his plans out of gear. Danger was imminent. Nevertheless, nothing in the world would have made him desert the Grange before his men returned.

They were due back at ten o'clock. They knew that the Grange would be evacuated by that hour and any who were unable to get home would make their own escape. Ten o'clock. There were three hours to go.

Storm, watching Zoeman's harassed expression, guessed at the conflicting emotions behind the smooth brow.

'Cheer up,' he murmured. 'You might get away with it yet. I have been known to fail. Hallo – this looks like trouble.'

Two men burst suddenly into the room. They had been running, for their breath came in great, quivering gasps.

'The Bugatti, Chief. Crashed into Wenlock's car. He's hiding behind Black Rock with a parcel of gunmen!'

The men in the Bugatti were smashed up! Storm felt a queasy sickness in his stomach as the realisation struck more deeply. Smashed up! Smashed up! The only chance of rescue from outside gone, and Grimm and Best gone with it. What accursed idiocy had made him send that letter instead of a wire or a telephone message? If Best and Grimm were dead it was his fault! If the others were murdered it was his fault!

He took a tight grip on himself as he watched the lynx-eyed leader of the English gang.

'Behind the Rock, are they?' muttered Zoeman. 'That means anyone coming in or going out will be under fire.' Despair touched him. *Redhead had attacked!* 'God! It will be massacre!'

'Whoa!' broke in Storm suddenly, his mind working at top speed. 'Wenlock doesn't know about your show down here, does he? At least, he doesn't know how to get in?'

'I don't think so,' admitted Zoeman.

'That means,' said Storm quickly, 'that he's planning on attacking us at the front. Me and my merry men, that is.'

'Well?'

Storm placed a hand on the smaller man's shoulder and spoke with a note of confidence, making Zoeman even more acutely aware of the iron determination and the utter lack of personal fear which characterised the engaging, likeable, obstinate and resourceful Martin Storm.

'Listen,' said Storm. 'We'll merge for a bit. Let me go out and wave a white flag. I'll tell him that you're here, and that I've got a message through to London and a whole army of police are on the way to smoke you out. If he bites and vamooses I want a free passage for myself and the others – and I'll undertake not to talk till, we'll say, nine o'clock. That'll give you three hours and more to get clear, because it'll take the police an hour to get down here if not more. After nine o'clock I'll be on your tail.'

'We will call it an armistice,' said Zoeman thoughtfully. 'But nine o'clock isn't late enough. Make it eleven.'

'Eleven has it,' said Storm.

'What happens if Wenlock doesn't see eye to eye with you?'

'I'll haul down the white flag,' chortled Storm, 'and sock him on the jaw. Suit you? Good. Send word to the others that there's still a chance of beer tonight. No – I'll leave the bandages till later. It'll look more impressive if they think I'm half-dead, and it's only a scratch anyhow.'

Ten minutes later Storm approached the drawbridge and through the gates could see the massive grandeur of Black Rock. No sound came from behind it and there was no sign of Wenlock and his men. With a step less sure than he would have liked – for he was feeling more pain from his wound than he confessed – he reached the centre of the road.

What was ahead? He knew, and grew sober at the realisation, that a bullet from Wenlock's gun would probably spell death. But there was just a chance that he might be able to scare the other man and, setting his lips grimly, he pressed on.

He wished the men behind Black Rock would speak. The silence was uncanny, turning him cold. Then suddenly;

'Keep still, Storm!'

It was Wenlock's rasping, cruel voice. It went on;

'What do you want?'

'Just a little chat.'

'Get back!' snarled Wenlock. 'Tell Zoeman I want to make a deal with him. Tell him that Redhead's due here at nine and, if he knows what's good for him, he'd better hurry.'

Storm swung round, chancing a bullet in his back. Wenlock knew that Zoeman was in possession of the Grange – but Wenlock wasn't Redhead!

He had suspected it but for the first time he knew. But there was one urgent, inescapable fact. Wenlock was either trying a cunning manoeuvre or – Storm admitted that it was a thousand times more likely – he was double-crossing the all-powerful Redhead!

18

Redhead Makes a Discovery

Sitting at a small table set for three the hunched, green-eyed, horrible figure of the gangster overlord faced Letty Granville. There was something devilish about that wizened, inhuman old man, a ghoulish gloating triumph turning his rasping laugh into a mutter of unspoken threats.

A hundred times during the meal she had repented her undertaking. Only the thought of Frank and the dire necessity for money would have made her do it – and now that she saw the malevolent evil in Redhead her heart went cold.

'Fifty thousand pounds, Miss Granville! A tremendous sum of money for a young girl and a lad.'

'We need it,' she said with an effort and looking at him squarely. 'And if it wasn't worth the money you would never have paid it.'

Redhead's thin lips cracked in a cackle of laughter.

'Sound logic, little lady, sound logic! Rare, too, in a pretty woman. And you made sure I didn't defraud you, didn't you?'

Letty knew nothing of the arrangements which Frank had made for the repayment of the money, but she took a chance.

'It was a matter of business.'

Redhead cackled again. The Granville fellow had made sure of getting his money after offering the plan of the Grange; Redhead had been forced to pay; there was no time for side-shows, for Zoeman was on the alert.

'Business, eh? Cash against documents! Very clever, very clever indeed. Don't you think so, Gazzoni?'

The Spanish-American forced a sickly grin and took his beady eyes from the slim beauty of the girl. The Granville dame had certainly 'got' him. It seemed a pity that she had to die.

'Sure, Boss,' he said without enthusiasm. 'Reckon you kin handle the jobs better'n me. But say – ' He leaned forward. 'Time's getting on. Nearly seven pips, Boss.' But he could not resist another leer in Letty Granville's direction.

Redhead's smile disappeared with disconcerting suddenness.

'Seven o'clock, is it? All right, Gazzoni. Phone through to the garage and make sure that it's all okay. I'll talk to the ship.'

In spite of the obvious devilry of his mind, Letty preferred Redhead in his rasping 'business' manner to his shuddering efforts at familiarity.

'Up to your room, Miss Granville. The old woman will release you at seven o'clock tomorrow morning.' He glowered down at her.

Gazzoni turned from the telephone as the door clicked behind the girl, his shifty eyes hooded.

'Garage all set, Boss.'

'Good. Go round and tell Rosselli I want the car.'

'Okay,' muttered Gazzoni. 'What about the girl?'

Redhead laughed.

'The old hag'll take her up supper tonight – doped. The hag's will be doped, too. Then Rosselli'll dump 'em both in the Dartmoor Bog.'

Gazzoni gave an answering snigger.

It was a pity the girl had to go, but it was wise. Trust Redhead to do the right thing.

Murder lurked over Letty Granville in the Park Street house. Cold, soulless murder.

To separate fifty thousand pounds apiece from men of the calibre of Redhead and Zoeman bespoke cleverness, but a crooked cleverness. Granville was clever and his mind tortuous. It was a near miracle that he had got away with it.

He needed the whisky and soda that he ordered at *The Four Bells*. Kurt, impassive and unspeaking, was standing next to him, his right hand in his mackintosh pocket, the gun in that hand uncomfortably near to Granville's stomach. His story, told briefly to the gaping Benjamin, went down well.

There was to be a war film taken in the grounds of Ledsholm Grange. And much though he regretted it the danger to spectators was so great that he would have to make sure that no-one from the village trespassed.

Mr Cripps understood very well, helped by the discreet passing, from Granville's hand to his, of a pound note. The village would keep away from Ledsholm Grange that night.

Granville left *The Four Bells* thinking with some satisfaction of the ease with which he had outwitted both Redhead and Zoeman. Storm had been easy, too.

But Storm was able to look after himself.

Leaving *The Four Bells* Granville climbed into the Daimler, acutely aware that the man sitting at the back of the car was holding a gun and that there was not the slightest chance of a getaway. Zoeman would keep a tight hold on him until the evacuation of Ledsholm Grange had been accomplished.

Granville went cold as he wondered what would happen if Zoeman knew the truth.

But for a scoop like this, risks had to be taken. Providing Letty got out of it with a whole skin he would have no regrets. He settled back in his seat, hardly noticing the stretch of dusty road in front of him until there was a sudden screech of brakes and a muttered curse from Kurt.

'What the hell – '

Granville looked ahead, stiff with horror.

In spite of the terrific force of the impact he recognised both the Bugatti and the Delage. The radiators and front parts were smashed to smithereens and the wreckage was scattered to a radius of twenty yards. But Granville had eyes only for the two battered and bloodstained men near the debris.

He recognised Grimm in a flash and after a moment's fear that the other was Storm, recognised the gravel-scarred face of Martin Best.

They had escaped and managed to get the Bugatti – only to crash into the Delage. And the Delage meant that Wenlock was about. *Wenlock, who knew of the double-crossing!*

Kurt's sharp voice rapped out.

'Do you recognise the other car?'

'Wenlock's,' muttered Granville.

Kurt looked at him queerly. Granville might have seen a ghost. In point of fact he had seen the hovering spectre of death which would open its gaping jaws quickly enough if Wenlock and Zoeman talked together.

With Granville's help the unconscious bodies of Grimm and Best were levered into the Daimler, and the car slid onward, its hawk-eyed driver keeping careful watch. Past the gleaming Black Rock they were in full view of Ledsholm Grange.

Granville felt like ice.

Zoeman was at the top of the steps, with Storm – and Wenlock!

Kurt turned the Daimler's nose towards the back of the house. Coming to a standstill in the courtyard he called out to a man on guard by the secret entrance to the underground quarters.

'What's happening, Hemmings?'

'Seems the Boss wants you, Kurt,' responded the other. 'And he wants Granville. Pow-wow of some kind.'

Granville was still in the Daimler, sliding from the seat next to the driver's to the open door. Kurt, looking round at him and watching Hemmings and another man lever the inert bodies of Grimm and Best from the back seats, snapped impatiently:

'Hurry, Granville.'

'Coming,' muttered the younger man, trying desperately to hide the panic in his eyes.

If Zoeman learned from Wenlock of the double-dealing there would be hell to pay! The tremendous efforts of the months, the scheming, the planning, the death-risking talk with Redhead all leading to the success which was within his grasp was trembling over the precipice of disaster.

Unless he could get away he was as good as dead. Zoeman could be as ruthless and merciless as Redhead.

Kurt was halfway to the kitchen door. Hemming and the second man had their hands full with Grimm and Best. There was one perilous chance – but the risk was better than certain death!

His hands pressed suddenly on the controls, sending the great Daimler into motion. If only he could get out of range before the tyres were pierced!

Driving like a man possessed he stepped on the accelerator, bent on the one desperate object – getaway. A bullet cracked through the bodywork at the back of the car. The bones of his hands shewed white through the skin.

Like spitting death the bullets streamed out, cracking against the wings, the bodywork, the lamps. Zig-zagging like a maniac he sent the car hurtling over flower beds and lawns on to the smooth surface of the drive. Steadying now that it was on a good road the Daimler leapt forward. Black Rock loomed up like a gaping monster but he wrenched his wheel round and skirted it by a fraction.

On the straight road he set the engine the biggest task of its short life. Seventy miles an hour! Eighty! Ninety! The shivering needle of the speedometer quivered like a mad puppet as the car raced on, a roaring monster of escape!

Kurt was one of the few men in Zoeman's organisation not in fear of his leader, but as he walked along the rubber-covered passage to the Chief's room his face was white and grim.

Zoeman was sitting at the table, with Wenlock opposite him and Storm on his right. The three American gunmen comprising Wenlock's bodyguard were in the room beyond, watched by silent but dangerous Englishmen.

Kurt lacked nothing in grit. He spoke quickly.

'Granville's made a break.'

Zoeman's eyes narrowed to mere slits.

'Didn't I tell you – '

'He didn't budge until we got back,' said Kurt quickly. 'We picked up a couple of Storm's men – alive but unconscious – and lugged them in the car. Granville must have seen you and Wenlock on the steps. He waited until we were getting Storm's men out, then raced off in the Daimler.'

Zoeman's fingers drummed on the table.

At first sight the getaway seemed the last straw, but on second thoughts it was for the best. Granville had ratted, had been playing a double game all along, and he had asked for death. But Zoeman had kept his hands clean of blood and he wanted to keep them that way.

Kurt saw the relaxing muscles of his face and breathed more freely.

'All right,' said Zoeman. 'Now listen to this.'

Kurt listened to the offer which Wenlock had made, and his lips curled. Yellowness and double-crossing were outside his range, and displays of it in others made him sneer.

He knew nothing of the hatred which the cunning, arrogant Wenlock had for Redhead. Wenlock had played second fiddle to his father and Gazzoni for years and all the repressed fires of his hatred boiled over. He wanted money and he wanted to save his own skin. The money he reckoned he could get from Zoeman for the sake of his knowledge of Redhead's plans. The safety he could get by informing the police of Ledsholm Grange. Zoeman would never conceive that he would squeal, but he knew that squealing was the only way of getting through without becoming a fugitive from the law for the rest of his life.

He told of the deal with Letty Granville – he had learned of the girl's return to the Park Street house from the old woman – of the plan to gain possession of the front of the Grange and blow down the wall of the wine-cellar in the one murderous swoop on the underground quarters, the time for it being set for half-past ten. Redhead knew nothing of the cunning eavesdropping by which he had gained this knowledge.

Zoeman waited until he had finished. Then:

'He won't take a chance on leaving his cars around too long. I fancy he'll be here just before the half-hour. Our men are due back at ten and we'll get clear straight away. Storm will take one car with his party, and after eleven o'clock he can do what he likes. We've got ten detachments back now and as soon as the stuff is loaded we'll send them out again. Kurt, you and Hemming will keep a watch on the road, and send the others off instead of letting them turn in here. I'll keep five men here with me, and send any strays after you. Got that?'

'All clear,' said Kurt grimly.

'Then get going.'

Zoeman stared at Storm grimly. He had no fears of failing to get clear once they were away from Ledsholm Grange. The proceeds of the great hold-up campaign would be divided between the members of the organisation, with a major share for himself, and once they were away from the Grange and the share-out had been made, it was each man for himself. And each man had secured a passport, had selected a route of escape.

Outside the room his men were shifting the vast hoard of money and jewels from the underground strong-room, loading them into cars ready for the great exodus. The greatest criminal enterprise in the history of England was reaching its climax!

Zoeman knew that he could trust Storm, and providing nothing else went wrong, he had a very fair chance of beating Redhead and the authorities.

Storm felt cold and fiercely miserable.

Granville's ratting he could have stood. But the thought that the girl had taken part in the treacherous enterprise turned him sick!

Redhead picked up the receiver and rasped into the mouthpiece. A second later his green eyes glittered with the satyrish venom that came so readily to them.

'Double-crossing, is he? Does he *dare!*'

Furiously he gave the *Utopia Garage* number and issued his orders.

'Get them moving, at once. I know it's two hours early, damn you! Get them moving! Is Rosselli there?'

'Yep.'

'Tell him to take these dames for a ride, and dump them just where I said.'

He swung round as Gazzoni opened the door, and in the mad fury of the moment sent the Italian cringing back.

'The kid's double-crossed us, Gazzoni! Vines followed him from the garage. He's down at the Grange, talking with Zoeman and Storm! We're starting now!'

'What about the girl?'

'We haven't time for dope. Crack their skulls, hers and the old woman's. Then get down to the ship with Rosselli!'

Five minutes later Letty heard the turning of the key in the lock. She swung round as the door opened.

Gazzoni was glaring at her hungrily.

'There ain't nothing to worry about, baby. Redhead reckoned you'd like to see this – '

His hand came from his pocket and for a ghastly second she saw the gleaming steel of a gun. His arm shot out and fixed her in a vice-like grip. With a sudden, frenzied strength she freed her right arm and struck him.

'You would, would you! That'll teach you, you little whelp!'

Something cracked against the back of her neck. Pain enfolded her, to be swallowed up in a whirring blackness as the revolver butt cracked again.

Unconscious, she sank down at the brute's feet.

Gazzoni stared down at her, wondering fearfully whether Redhead had heard the scuffle. Redhead had ordered silence.

Darting to the small window he looked out into the street in time to see the tail-end of the Packard car which Redhead was using for his journey to the Grange. That was all right. Now he had to wait for Rosselli, after he'd dealt with the old woman in the downstairs room.

He was with her within five minutes, and the terrible fear in her eyes brought a maniacal cackle to his cruel lips. The butt of his gun rose and fell.

Once – twice – thrice –

Gazzoni stopped suddenly. He had heard nothing, had felt nothing, had seen nothing. But he swung round –

A bullet winged its message of death across the room, sending the dago staggering back. A second bit into his chest. He lurched, falling over the stretched body of the old woman.

Death had taken Gazzoni.

At the door of the kitchen Frank Granville stared at the two lifeless bodies, with a terrible sickness at his heart. For a second he had thought the woman on the floor to be Letty. Surely Redhead hadn't taken her?

He had watched Redhead go out, and could have sworn that the man had been alone with the chauffeur of the Packard. Surely Letty was there.

He found her three minutes later. Feeling for her heart he discovered that she was still alive. In a trice he had whipped out a flask of whisky and set it to her lips.

Watching, waiting, he saw her stir. Her eyes opened.

'Frank!'

He spoke nervously.

'Steady a minute, Letty. We've pulled it off, but we'll have to clear out, and clear out smartly.'

He helped her to her feet and felt a rush of exhilaration as she managed to walk unsteadily to the door. He had torn her out of Redhead's clutches. Now they had to make good their escape. He thanked the fates for the Daimler which was waiting outside a house several doors along the street.

19

A FUSION OF FORCES

The twins stared aghast at the huge, bandaged figure of Martin Storm as he stepped blithely from the passage into their midst.

Righteous swung round like a bucking horse.

'Damnation, Windy! We thought you were clear!'

'Well, I'm not,' grinned Storm.

The four luckless members of the party of optimistic young men who had been overcome by the gas had been overwhelmed later in the day while keeping the stations which Storm had allotted to them. They were consoling themselves with the thought that Storm, Best and Grimm had got clear and that in the attack by Zoeman's men they had managed to inflict more than a bit of damage.

They retained a faith born of experience in the ability of Martin Storm to pull the game off. And the sight of his great body framed in the doorway with a stolid faced gunman in the offing gave them a nasty jolt.

'But what – ' began Dodo.

'Armistice,' announced Storm. 'Follow me, and I'll explain all. And don't start looking warlike, Tim. The cove behind is peaceable but he's got a gun for all that.'

Back in the room in which Zoeman held court, Storm spoke at length and with some feeling on the affairs to date. The fact that both Grimm and Best were comparatively well and kicking had done a great deal to ease his mind.

'Taking it square and round, it's deadlock,' he told them. 'For the time being Zoeman is giving us a run. Wenlock has ratted on Redhead, but for which charming piece of double-dealing we'd have been in the soup. At the moment he is in the strong-room. As soon as we're clear and ready to go he'll be freed. Lord help us, bribery and corruption isn't in it! Fifty thousand pounds Zoeman's given to Wenlock for the information, and fifty thousand he's given to that little runt Granville – '

The twins, Righteous and Dodo stared at him aghast.

'Granville?' ejaculated Tobias. 'But – '

Storm's face went grim.

'Granville's broke, or nearly broke. That's why he came back to England sooner than he was expected. He struck a deal with Zoeman and knew all along that the Grange was a rogues' meeting hall, so to speak. That poor blighter Harries wasn't lying; the wireless station was the story that Granville put about.

'But he wasn't satisfied with the cash from Zoeman. He's also worked in with Redhead for a nice packet of oof. Redhead's got a plan of the Grange, which plan Granville gave to his sister.

'Miss Granville,' went on Storm with an effort, 'closed a deal with Redhead. Redhead's due to make a mass attack at half-past ten. But knowing it, Zoeman's planning to get clear before the firing starts. His stuff – cash and gems and the Lord knows what – is being packed into cars up above and there'll be a move pretty soon. For a while, though, Zoeman, a few of his thugs and us, will hang on here, until the rest of his merry men get back. That'll be at ten o'clock. After that we all sheer off, and we let Zoeman have a few hour's run before we lodge any information. That's the whole story, lads.'

It was a remarkable fact that none of them had any fears about the wisdom of relying on Zoeman's words.

The twins looked at each other and yawned. Righteous Dane shrugged his shoulders wearily. Dodo Trale and Storm, tired beyond belief, dropped into chairs.

A few seconds later they were more tensely alert than ever before.

Zoeman was approaching with short, hurried steps. He pushed the door wide open and they saw by his face that there was trouble.

'Storm,' he snapped, 'we're in a hell of a tight fix. *Redhead's outside!*'

Storm stared, aghast.

'He's in the grounds,' Zoeman went on hurriedly. 'The first car was going out when it was overturned, smashed into the drawbridge after Kurt and the others in it were shot up. From what I can see he's keeping a watch on the roads *and nothing can get in or get out!* We can't get the stuff back into the strong-room – it would be too risky. We'll have to fight for it!'

Storm's eyes glinted.

'What about the dynamite business in the wine-cellar?'

'If they can get through the front hall,' said Zoeman grimly, 'we're finished.' He eyed Storm squarely. 'Well – are you fighting?'

There was a certain restlessness about those four battle-scarred ornaments to society immediately behind Martin Storm.

He grinned.

'Yes, we're fighting. But it can't last long.'

'Why?' demanded Zoeman.

'Hang it,' said Storm, 'the whole countryside – '

Then for the first time he learned of the precaution which Zoeman had taken to keep suspicion away from the coming and going of his fleet of cars. A war film! God!

'Spread some guns round,' he said suddenly. 'It's bad, but it might be worse. You want us to keep the front hall?'

'Yes. I'll lend you half-a-dozen men when we're clear out here.'

'How many car-loads of stuff have you got up there?'

'Five,' said Zoeman. And his right hand shot out.

'I'll take you!' grinned Storm.

They stared at each other for a moment as they shook hands, and for the first time neither man was challenging nor mocking. It was a fusion of forces.

Redhead was outside. They knew that his armoury included machine-guns, and they knew the effect of a sweeping hail of bullets. Besides which the crowning irony of the carefully conceived plans which Zoeman had made to allay suspicion in the people of Ledsholm village doubled the odds against them. Ledsholm Grange was isolated, right away from the beaten track, a perfect island of terror to come.

Four hundred yards away from the main hall they saw half-a-dozen men at the gates of the draw-bridge. A large car – they had no doubt it was steel-plated – was moving slowly towards the front of the Grange. A second, just as heavily built, was crawling towards the rear of the great house, and behind each were half-a-dozen men.

Several cars, innocent-looking machines but fitted with super-charged engines, were drawn up in the road outside Black Rock, while the wreckage of the ill-fated Kurt's car was still blocking part of the drive.

A perfect scene for a film.

A hell of a scene for true life!

Silently they stood, as the heavily-built engine moved remorselessly forward. It was the start of the attack, of the ruthless, cold-blooded murder which was to come.

20

ATTACK!

Along the winding drive of the Grange the car approached.

What was in that heavily constructed car? What would be Redhead's first move?

The answer was not slow in coming. A lead-nosed bullet flashed through a window, biting into the oak sideboard which had been pushed into the breach.

'Rifles,' muttered Storm.

'Trouble,' murmured Dodo.

Fast upon their words came a fusillade of bullets. There was no sound of firing, only the cracking thud of the messengers of death against the barricade, a ceaseless barrage of rifle fire defying them to poke their noses into danger, keeping them tight-lipped away from the line of fire.

Through a small chink in the sideboard Storm took advantage of a momentary lull. Outside he could see nothing but three cars drawn up at the foot of the stone steps. He swung round quickly.

'They're here. Snipe them if it's only their toes!'

The words were hardly out of his mouth when something crashed against the great oak door. A short lull was followed by a second crash.

'A battering ram,' muttered Storm, and took a firmer grip of his gun.

Behind any piece of furniture that afforded cover the five men crouched tensely, fingers on the triggers of their guns.

Again the battering ram smashed into the door, sending a deep crack from top to bottom. Then the relentless attack quickened, with battering ram no longer moving in measured lunges but hitting the door with short, calculated lunges as the crack widened. Through it Storm caught sight of a face. His finger touched the trigger of his gun.

'One,' he muttered, overcoming a wave of nausea.

The madness of it! Four miles away in the village of Ledsholm they were talking lightly of the film! And it was a fight to the bitter end!

Under another shattering onslaught the crack widened to a foot. Storm's gun spoke again, followed by a stab of yellow flame from Dodo Trale's automatic. Outside a hoarse, pain-driven curse and a horrible rasping gurgle split the low-toned hum of talk.

'Two,' murmured Trale, tight-lipped.

'Get ready for a rush,' warned Storm.

For the last time the battering ram smashed into the stout oak, crashing down the last shiver of resistance. Above the roaring madness of noise Storm heard:

'Now get 'em!'

And through the cloud of dust still flying upwards he saw a dozen quick-footed men streaming into the hall. His gun spoke twice. The first bullet reached its mark, the second missed.

With miraculous speed one of the gansters lifted a machine-gun to his shoulder. A dozen bullets bit into the leather of the settee.

Storm crouched behind it, not daring to risk another shot while that hail of bullets stormed towards him. But Dodo was out of range and his gun belched fire. Once – twice – thrice! The man with the machine-gun doubled up, shot through the heart.

Storm's gun spoke again. From right and left the others followed suit, sending a regular hail of spitting death into the small crowd of gunmen standing within the threshold. Cursing, screaming, diving for safety, the crowd split up.

Leaning against the wall as he reloaded his automatic Storm called out softly:

'First trick to us. Anyone hurt?'

'Nothing serious – look out!'

Dodging back behind the settee Storm could see the tip of a machine-gun just above the level of the top step. Without warning it began to spit fire. A stream of bullets hummed into the hall, sweeping along the floor, the range gradually getting higher. Badly bitten by their first effort the attackers had learned caution.

'Hell!' muttered Storm.

The whining horror of the machine-gun bullets set up a wail that would have struck fear into the heart of the Devil himself. Against the bottom of the settee and the chairs behind which the defenders crouched the terrible tap-tap-tap set up a pecking rhythm which they knew could not last long before penetrating their barricades.

'Load up,' urged Storm in a harsh undertone, 'and fire at the gun. All together, mind you. All ready – now!'

With sudden biting ferocity the five automatics spat out. The nozzle of the machine-gun jerked upwards, then the whole thing split asunder. The gun dropped from sight on to the heads of the gangsters.

'Massacre, wouldn't you say, Windy?' Timothy Arran murmured.

'Nothing to what it will be if they break through,' swore Storm grimly. 'Anyhow, that's twice we've beaten 'em. I wonder – damnation! What was that?'

As he spoke there came a tremendous explosion from the back of the Grange. Quick upon it came a low throated rumbling, striking the fear of uncertainty into their hearts.

'Trouble at the back,' cursed Storm. 'Don't move, Tim! The cusses haven't finished at the front yet. Ah! I thought so!'

His gun spat viciously and a cautiously raised head dropped out of sight. His mind was working quickly. Providing the attackers didn't use bombs to get them away the five men in the hall could keep going.

The thing was, what had happened to Zoeman?

There was something pleasing in the handshake with Storm. It gave Zoeman a strange feeling of buoyancy, in spite of the danger from outside.

Hemmings, who had taken over Kurt's job as second-in-command, swung into the hall suddenly.

'They've got armoured cars, Boss. Not a doubt about it.'

'Rifles or revolvers?' demanded Zoeman.

'Both,' grimaced Hemmings.

'Right. Get everyone under cover. They won't come too close, but if you get a chance, shoot to kill.'

Shoot to kill!

Hemmings knew that 'no killing' had been the strictest order that Zoeman had ever given. His words, spoken coolly but with chilling intensity, meant that they were in the absolute last line of defence.

He swung out of the room, snapping instructions to men who passed him as he ran up the stairs. A dozen men were crouching in the courtyard, taking advantage of every possible piece of cover. The five treasure-cars were being guarded to the death!

Help, unless it came from the police and in vast numbers, was impossible. Redhead had got a stranglehold. The only possible chance was to tire the attackers and choose the right moment for a sortie.

Darting about the courtyard the men – there were less than twenty at the Grange – were rigging up barricades to make sure that the vulnerable parts of the treasure-cars escaped damage. A hundred yards ahead, out of range of revolver fire, the slowly advancing monster of a car was creeping –

A desultory fire of rifle shots kept them fully alive to the danger of revealing themselves. Three men had already been killed, and as Hemmings dashed towards the power-house a bullet flattened against the wall. From behind him a man gasped and threw up his arms.

'Four,' muttered Hemmings, and shuddered.

He had never believed the monstrous stories of the ruthless killings which shocked the United States from end to end. He had scoffed at Redhead. He had known nothing of the machine-like devilry with which Redhead killed. He was hard-bitten so far as crime in England went, but the horror of this attack sent his blood to fever-heat.

He realised that the very care which Zoeman had taken to lull suspicion was now reacting against them, and that nothing and no-one, could stop this mass murder.

Quietly and placidly the countryside was settling down for the night, mildly titillated by the sounds they took to be those of a film battle.

Hemmings felt the footsteps of the living walking over his grave!

He issued orders quickly and effectively. The five cars with their load of wealth were ready for flight when the moment came for that desperate sortie. Glass splintered suddenly.

Straining his eyes Hemmings stared towards the first of the armoured cars driven by a man whose face was barely visible.

'Keep a close watch,' he ordered. 'I'll tell Zoeman.'

Zoeman heard Hemmings out without speaking. Then:

'So they're getting nearer. I'll come up. Bring that last case with you and then send six men round to the front. Storm'll be in a tight fix, I fancy.'

Zoeman rushed up the stairs quickly. At the top he saw the desperate backward glances of the men manning the boarded window.

'It looks mighty bad, Chief.'

Careful not to show himself Zoeman went to the window. For the first time he saw the monstrous armoured car, and his lips tightened as he watched it moving forward like a great crab, its blunt nose turned towards the kitchen door.

'No driver,' muttered Zoeman. 'I wonder what they're up to?'

Slowly, horribly, the great crab-like leviathan crept towards them. Like men paralysed they stared in chilled fascination and bewilderment.

Then Zoeman saw it!

Whipping round like a maniac he shouted to Hemmings:

'Get all the men inside and down to the cellars! Hurry! Get them out of the power-house, the sheds, and out of here!'

Befuddled but obedient, Hemmings swung round, but as he turned he caught sight of the car which had gained a sudden leaping momentum. He stood dead still, stiff with fear and a gripping horror. The fearful contraption was less than five yards from the power-house. As he watched it crashed against a corner stone.

Something leapt out of the radiator. The great car reared up on its back wheels. Swinging round from the power-house it leapt towards the main building, and as the great bulk crashed into the wall a ghastly thunder of explosion roared into the heavens. Hemmings gave a strangled cry as he saw flame shooting from the fearful mass. Bricks, stones and mortar crashed downwards in a dust-raising bellowing medley, as the wall caved in with a thunderous roar. Hemmings, miraculously unhurt, went sick as he saw the mangled form of the man who had been standing nearest the window tossed high into the air.

The shattered brickwork thundered about him as he staggered blindly towards the hole in the inner wall which led to the underground refuge. He came upon Zoeman suddenly, dishevelled and white-faced, appearing out of a cloud of thick, choking dust.

'I'm going to tell Storm,' gasped Zoeman. 'Get below, keep the door open and shoot the swine down!'

Hemmings staggered towards the startled men climbing up the debris-strewn stairs.

'Explosives!' he rasped hoarsely. 'Get back – '

Dazed and bemused he saw Ralph Wenlock's sandy skin and flaming red hair as Redhead's son darted out of the strong-room. But he was intent only on keeping the coming attack at bay and he brushed past the man.

Wenlock swung round. The explosion had broken the electric control of the strong-room doors and he had dashed in fear to discover the cause of the trouble. For a terrible moment he realised that Redhead had come earlier than expected; Redhead's awful green eyes seemed to glower before him. He saw the gaping jaws of certain death.

His mind caught desperately to the one chance of escape from his father's damnable vengeance. He hurried into the strong-room and spoke quickly to the three thugs who had joined him in the double-cross.

'Redhead! He's blown the top of the place to pieces. Go for the first man you see, get his gun. We can hold out now – *for Redhead!*'

His men saw the cunning of the manoeuvre. Zoeman and his bandits would be between two fires once they were armed.

The man Greenaway, hurriedly refilling his automatic, saw them when it was too late. Wenlock's fist, clenched with the fury of fear and hope, crashed into his stomach. His gun dropped to the floor. Wenlock grabbed the weapon and touched the trigger.

Greenaway's last breath rattled in his throat.

Storm heard the urgent tapping on the door leading to the hall from the back of the Grange and darted towards it. Then he dropped back, aghast.

Zoeman was there. Blood was streaming down his forehead, dust and dirt was in his hair and on his clothes; but the steely glint in his grey eyes was like granite.

'Get your men downstairs, Storm. They've blown a hole in the wall. I'm afraid of fire!'

Creeping carefully until they were out of range they made their way to the rear of the Grange. From there they watched Redhead's men approaching cautiously.

'Here's a chance,' muttered Storm. 'One by one, you fellows. We'll have a shy at 'em.'

Keeping well back he took careful aim towards the dozen men creeping towards the breach in the wall. One man staggered back.

Timothy Arran, the last of the five men, was halfway across the kitchen when Storm saw for a second time a hunched, wizened old man with glowing green eyes. He had seen him before in the Delage when they had rescued Letty Granville from the Park Street house. There was something sinister in those awful eyes, even at that distance.

At last! Redhead! That old man with the satyrish eyes – Redhead!

He took aim and fired. The flying bullet hummed towards its object. The satyr staggered backwards, his hands clutching his chest. Three or four gunmen crowded round him.

'God!' exulted Storm. *I've got him!*'

Then Redhead moved like a great ape, lurching out of the line of fire. Storm went cold. Was the man immune from death?

He had fired at the gangster baron's heart – but between the monster's flesh and the lead-nosed bullet was a bullet-proof steel chain!

Storm cursed himself for a fool. He should have realised that the man would take this elementary precaution, and aimed for the head instead of the heart. But the damage was done. He had lost a golden opportunity.

Zoeman spoke with an effort.

'We shall need a miracle to get us out of this.'

'One never knows.' Storm returned, breaking off as something pecked into his hand.

He looked down, seeing it wet with blood.

Three steps below them Wenlock, his automatic still smoking from the shot, was grinning upwards in malevolent triumph.

'Come down, Storm. I've been waiting for this.'

The very imminence of the danger steadied Storm's nerves. He could laugh in the face of death.

'What-ho! Ginger! Shouldn't waggle that pea-shooter about too much, in case it goes off. How's your father?'

Before he could speak again he saw Zoeman's white lips as the older man looked towards the gaping hole blown in the wall by the explosion. Swinging round he found himself gazing into the basilisk orbs of the hunched Redhead!

'Redhead!' he breathed, and his voice was cracked and dry.

Saul Wenlock lurched forward. A dozen men behind him showed their guns, rendering him safe from attack. For the first time he was face to face with the man who had done most to thwart his plans.

The realisation flashed across Storm's mind like forked lightning. Redhead, the man whose identity had puzzled the police of two nations, was Saul Wenlock, chief of the Wenlock Oil Corporation!

Loathsome, unclean, diabolic, all the sin in the world emanated from him, forming that fearful aura of frightfulness which hovered about him. Redhead, the foulest horror of America's era of crime. Redhead, the man whose thin lips opened to spell death!

He stared like a fiend from hell. The mocking coolness of Storm's eyes seemed to infuriate him. His gross body shook.

'So you are Storm. Well – you have just five minutes to live.'

Storm felt cold. That was not a threat. It was a fact. Redhead had planned his death and the manner of it would be worse than death itself. His muscles tightened, but he was weak from loss of blood. As Redhead's cruel lips opened again he staggered.

'Get him!' snapped Redhead.

Something broke in Storm's mind. He hurtled forward into the mass of gangsters, his great arms whirling like flails. Men gasped, fell back, shrieked oaths and returned to the fight. A dozen gunmen crushed on him, beating his resistance down, sending torture through his body.

Zoeman leapt forward, but a bullet from Redhead's gun took him in the thigh. Two men carried him towards the armoured car which was drawn up in the courtyard amidst the debris of that first terrific explosion and the wreckage of five treasure-cars which had gone up with the rest, scattering the wealth of a nation about the courtyard.

Storm, and Zoeman too, were carried to a car, the door slammed and locked on them. Through the narrow window Wenlock's ghastly cackle reached them.

'Storm! Zoeman! Both where I want you! You'll live long enough to see the first of the stuff brought up – the five million pounds that you thought was yours! It's mine, all mine! But before it's loaded you'll split the sky! You're sitting on dynamite!'

Forcing his voice to a quiet strength Storm answered him.

'So we'll split the heavens, will we? *So did your share of the money, Redhead!* You're treading on it now!'

Slowly, devilishly, Redhead lit a match. The realisation that his coup had failed turned him to an ice-cold devil. His body shook as he began to wreak his vengeance.

The flame caught the white trail of fuse leading from the petrol tank of the car and as it spluttered he drew back. It was Satan who glared madly through his eyes and passed sentence of ghastly death.

'Five minutes, Storm!'

21

EXCITEMENT IN HIGH CIRCLES

Sir William Divot looked at the Prime Minister and from him to the keen-eyed member of that little known but extremely powerful 'Z' Department.

'I have just had a telephone message from Ledsholm village, Sir John. It is believed that a – er – film is to be taken at Ledsholm Grange tonight.'

The Home Secretary who was also the Premier turned his iron grey head towards the 'Z' Department agent. He was more worried about Redhead than he cared to acknowledge. All day reports had been received of outrage after outrage. He could see no end to it.

'Do you know about that, Number Twelve?'

The young man nodded jerkily.

'Yes, sir. The story was spread round in case of trouble. I've given a full report to Number One asking for immediate action. But there should be enough men down there to cope with it. My report went through early.'

The Prime Minister committed an indiscretion. He mentioned the name of the chief of 'Z' Department.

'Craigie is down with malaria. He's had a bad turn.'

He stared aghast at the leaping horror in the eyes of Number Twelve. The agent's face was aflame with living dread.

'My God! He's not been working all day?'

'He's been unconscious most of the time,' said the Prime Minister with considerable irritation.

Number Twelve looked crazed.

'God! Redhead's down there – and the job's been left! Storm – Best – Grimm – God! I thought it was all covered. We were going to mass forces outside Ledsholm – '

The Prime Minister looked scared.

'I'd better get in touch with the Chief Constable. We weren't expecting developments yet – '

Number Twelve crashed his fist down on the table.

'There isn't time for getting in touch! You've got to issue instructions! Damnation! It'll be massacre!'

'Steady,' murmured Sir William Divot.

Number Twelve swung round furiously. Statesmen meant nothing – hell was brewing at Ledsholm.

'Steady? We've got to act! Get the Flying Squad – get an armed force! Redhead's armed to the teeth – machine-guns – bombs – armoured cars! We were only waiting for the time to strike. I gave it in my report. Good God, sir, can't you – ?'

The Premier's hand was touching the telephone when the bell burred out. He went to a second instrument as Sir William Divot lifted it to his ear. A moment later he swung round in livid fear.

'It's Number Seven speaking, sir, from Ledsholm. Redhead's there! He's cut the telephone wires in the village – he's shooting –'

'Give it to me,' snapped the Premier. 'Hallo – hallo – '

He pumped uselessly at the telephone, the blood draining from his face. There was no voice at the other end.

Number Twelve read disaster in that white face.

His voice trembled as he spoke.

'I'm going down there. But for God's sake hurry with help – armed forces!'

He raced out of the room and down the steps of Number 10, Downing Street, heedless of the startled policeman on duty as he leapt towards a waiting saloon car containing a solitary passenger. His fingers were on the self-starter before he spoke hoarsely.

'Craigie's ill – and it's started!'

His passenger went icily cold as the great car raced through the streets of London, making for the Great West Road at a speed which brought a dozen policemen's hands to their notebooks before they noticed the all-important number-plate which signalled the Flying Squad sign in emergency. For the first time 'Z' Department's plans had fallen through!

At Number 10, Downing Street, a white-faced Premier was talking urgently to a Man Who Mattered at the War Office.

22

Toby Arran Takes a Chance

Death hovered in the courtyard of Ledsholm Grange.

The terrible chaos created by the terrific explosion of the first hell-loaded car held the torn limbs of men and the shredded papers of half-a-million of money. And it held the awful Redhead. Storm shivered as he looked through the small window of the car.

The thought uppermost in his mind was that the devil had netted Letty Granville into his campaign of money-lust and blood-letting. If he could only get his fingers round the thick neck of that red-haired, green-eyed monster he would laugh in mad glory as the life was choked out of him.

It was his helplessness which sent his blood to fire and his heart like a battering ram against his ribs. His face worked convulsively and for a while he kept his eyes from Zoeman. He could realise the ghastly horror of the other man's mind. Zoeman was living in the hell of his own creating yet he had created it unwillingly.

It was impossible for them to escape from that armoured car of death in which they were imprisoned. The windows, fitted with unbreakable glass, were mere slits; they were imprisoned in their tomb of steel.

For the last time Storm saw the basilisk green eyes of the monstrous Redhead, saw the evil leer on the wizened, sinstained face, heard the maniacal cackle from the thick throat. Then Redhead stepped out of sight into the safety of the underground vaults.

Storm knew that the devil could never get away with it. His enormous vanity and near insanity would prove his undoing. But when help came it could spell only retribution. It would be too late to stop the evil he had done.

Storm stared backwards, through the glass slit in the back of the car. Above it a light spiral of smoke curled from the burning fuse which was creeping with terrible slowness towards the dynamite-filled petrol tank. If only he could break the glass!

In a sudden frenzy of helplessnes he crashed his fist into the unyielding panel, feeling nothing. Madly he rammed, madly, helplessly, frenziedly.

Zoeman's strained voice stopped him.

'It's no use, Storm. I'm – sorry – '

Storm gulped and the cloud of frenzy cleared from his brain, swept by an ice-cold blast of sanity. He looked down on his bruised and blood-red hand with a half-foolish grin.

'Darned silly, what? Oh Lord, don't worry, Zoeman. I wouldn't mind scrapping with you again.'

Zoeman opened his lips to speak but before the words came gave one startled gasp of horror.

'My God!'

Storm, his face working, saw the demolished door of the secret passages filled for a moment with an unrecognisable bundle. Then something was hurtled into the courtyard – something human!

It was Martin Best, heaved by two of the devils who worked for the satyr below. Best's face cracked against the rubble as a second figure hurtled upwards.

'Grimm,' muttered Storm, and his tongue lashed the murky air of the car with a stream of invective which spat uselessly against the surrounding steel. 'The ruddy devil's sending them all up here – all of them!'

He was right. Downstairs the six remaining members of the party which had rushed cheerfully to the 'beano' two days before had been overwhelmed by the attacks from front and behind. One by one they had been hurled through the gaping hole in the wall, while Redhead savoured his insatiable thirst for vengeance.

Toby Arran was the last man up and he saw the inert bodies about him with a groan. Straining his head round he saw the haggard face of Martin Storm in the car.

The grin that he sent across the five yards of space between them was one of the bravest things he ever did. Storm saw it and felt a sudden crazy exultation.

He saw Toby's lips move and saw Dodo Trale squirm over on his back, his face covered in blood. Still the curl of smoke rose from the spluttering fuse.

Would that last moment never come? The waiting was sending him mad, sending the blood racing like molten lava through his veins, bringing a ghastly lump to his throat which choked him – choked him –

Toby Arran was cursing, coldly and with blood-curdling intensity.

'If I can get this blankety blank rope on that blankety piece of glass I'll tear my blinking blankety wrists into blazing shreds but I'll tear the scorching tongue of that redheaded, green-goggled cackle-throated he-devil and squeeze his foul breath out of his blankety body till he shrieks for ruddy mercy! Can I? Oh, my God! Can I?'

Dodo watched, the blood frozen in his veins. He could see the grey ash of the fuse and the glowing red spark less than an inch from the petrol tank. If it lasted another minute before sending hell into the heavens it would be a miracle.

'One minute – fifty seconds – '

Toby Arran was staring at the glowing red spark, his eyes blazing and his face working convulsively as he lacerated his wrists on the sharp-edged piece of glass beneath him.

The rope round his wrists sagged.

Forty seconds –

A wild exultation surged through him as the rope snapped! He squirmed round, grabbing that heaven-sent piece of glass and sawing madly through the ropes at his ankles. Once – twice – thrice – he smashed on to the breaking threads.

Thirty seconds. Half a minute –

Staggering drunkenly he reached his feet, swaying from side to side. The little red glow of the fuse seemed to surge backward and forwards before his straining eyes, a little red ember of fearful death. He lurched towards it, unconscious of the hope-tightened faces of Storm and Zoeman through the glass, crazily aware only of the fuse, forcing his mind to act, forcing himself forward.

Twenty seconds –

The white fuse showed a bare quarter of an inch from the petrol tank. His fingers searched shakily along the smooth surface, creeping with terrifying slowness towards the spark. His head was whirling, his stomach heaving, his whole body was stiff and cold. Then through the mist in his mind he heard Storm's voice, firm and clear.

'Good boy, Toby!'

Arran gulped and his mind cleared for a split-second. In that second his forefinger and thumb darted towards the red spark, caught it firmly and squeezed, heedless of the burning pain scorching through his arm, heedless of everything but the one overwhelming fact. He had pulled it off!

He waved his arms in crazy exultation for a mad moment before he dropped unconscious on the rubble-strewn yard.

Reprieve!

The thing seemed incredible! Storm gulped as he saw Toby's blackened thumb and finger.

For the moment they were safe. But Toby was down and Dodo Trale was bound hand and foot. Dodo was dragging himself madly towards the lump of jagged glass. Tight-lipped and feverish-eyed Storm saw him repeating Arran's manoeuvre.

Then he shouted a useless warning. Through the hole in the wall he saw the demonaic eyes of Redhead, green, fiendish, glowing with the blood-lust which possessed him.

Redhead was staring horribly at the moving Trale and the inert body of Arran. He realised now why the explosion had been delayed. His lips cracked open.

'Get me a gun!'

Storm went cold. Toby's effort – Dodo's effort – all useless. Redhead's spidery hand was thrust behind him.

Then the heavens seemed to split in a droning roar. Something dark winged across the sky, its engine roaring as it slowed down and the aeroplane searched for a landing place.

He saw a figure outlined against the gleaming metal of the plane, a man standing perilously on the wing, a man whose right hand was pointing downwards –

And he saw the sudden spit of flame from the automatic gripped in the airman's hand.

A bullet hummed downwards. Staring upwards, Redhead seemed paralysed by this unthought of interruption. He hardly realised that a man was standing on the wing, hardly saw the tiny spurt of flame from the gun before something cracked into his skull, and he dropped backwards into the men who were crowding through a hole in the wall.

Storm felt a crazy exultation surging through him. He saw that spurt of red from Redhead's splintered skull before he peered upwards again.

The dare-devil airman was climbing steadily into the cockpit of the double-controlled Moth, which swooped suddenly upwards. Storm had seen him, and one word spat from his lips with incredible joy, making him oblivious to the sudden roaring filling the air, the dozen fighting planes which were winging their way towards the Grange.

One word!

'Granville!'

Then Zoeman, white-faced but with a tight-lipped smile, said softly:

'Granville. And he's brought plenty of support. God! Look at them running!'

Redhead's men were scuttling madly, helplessly, hope-lessly towards the Black Rock and the fleet of cars. But they stopped in terror as a vast explosion roaring through the air shot a mountain of blasted earth upwards.

Bombs!

Redhead was dead – and Redhead had failed!

Then Zoeman spoke again.

'Yes, it was Granville. But did you see his pilot?'

'No,' admitted Storm tensely.

'Also Granville,' said Zoeman simply. 'His sister!'

23

MARTIN STORM STARTS
A JOURNEY

'Where,' demanded a bandaged but spruce Timothy Arran who arrived last at a meeting of many cheerful, not to say boisterous young men at Martin Storm's Audley Street flat, 'is our heroine?'

Martin Storm was unable to suppress the mild flush which coloured his rugged face as he tried to look unconcerned.

Frank Granville, boisterously welcomed earlier in that evening ten days after the attack on Redhead, spoke for the silent Martin.

'She's gone for a rest cure, you men. Just outside Torquay, if you must know where.'

'If she wants peace and quiet,' grinned someone, 'take a tip from me and don't let Windy know where she's gone.'

Storm, busy with a number of brightly gleaming tankards, had time enough to heave a cushion neatly into the speaker's midriff.

'Oi! Here – '

Storm dodged its return with a grin.

'Now then, comrades and brothers, collect your liquor and let's get down to it.'

The barrel was rapidly emptying when there came a modest knock on the door.

'A telegram for Mr Granville, sir.'

There was silence as Granville split the envelope. Then:

'The Prime Minister,' announced Granville, 'says talk, but talk with discretion.'

'Start at once,' suggested Storm.

Granville, stuffing the telegram in his pocket, shrugged his shoulders.

'When all's said and done,' he pointed out, 'there isn't a great deal to tell. But to start at the beginning – '

'It isn't generally known that my father was prominent behind the scenes in diplomatic circles, and for a long time he worked in conjunction with "Z" Department. It was not an accident when he and my mother were killed; they were murdered by a pretty gang of scoundrels, and I had more than a suspicion of the truth. I got in touch with Gordon Craigie.

'There wasn't a great deal I could do, but unknown to Letty I sent despatches about various places and people while we were travelling. One particular job called for a nasty bit of handling and I was more lucky than clever. Anyhow, after it was finished I had orders to go to America and keep an eye on Redhead.

'I had to give some excuse for being away from Letty for days, sometimes weeks, at a time, so I told her that I was playing the markets. Then trouble began to fall thick and fast. Redhead knew that someone was watching him, and I was given information about the gang outrages in London.

'Gangs have to have headquarters. I advertised the Grange, and again with a large slice of luck got Zoeman's reply. I fixed things with him – and then heard that Wenlock was also keen on getting the place. That put me in a spot, because only Letty could help me, and I was anxious not to let her know anything about "Z" Department. Wenlock threatened trouble unless I went with him to England – and fixed Ledsholm Grange for him. Again I had to make up a story to tell Letty – she didn't know that I'd let the Grange – and I told her that I'd been losing heavily.

'She took it well. But I didn't expect Wenlock would cart her off when we reached the Grange, and when he did I was in a fix – I wanted to keep in with both Zoeman and Wenlock, of course, in an effort to get them caught in the same net. I'd already managed to interest Storm and Grimm, and I sent that wire, in the hope of keeping Letty out of danger.

'But I didn't reckon on them being quite so wide awake for trouble. I didn't see a ghost of a chance of getting both Redhead and Zoeman together while they were at the Grange – Storm and Grimm, I mean – so I took a desperate chance and got Letty to give that note to Redhead instead of taking it myself. I was still expecting to get rid of you fellows by that stunt, but again it didn't come off. You know that I had to look after her myself, and not only came precious near being too late but nearly missed learning that Craigie had been taken ill and that you were in a pretty serious plight at the Grange. As soon as I heard of this, I dashed off to Heston – Letty was in the Daimler outside – chartered a plane, which I knew Letty could pilot, and just managed to pull it off. The men at Whitehall had worked pretty quickly and sent a dozen bombers as well as a fleet of Flying Squad cars. Generally speaking you know the rest.'

He took a long swig at his beer. Storm grinned.

'God! It was a sight seeing those johnnies dashing round. I'll never be able to tell you how glad I was when you flew over, Granny.'

'And me!' said Dodo Trale fervently.

'And Zoeman,' put in Storm quietly. 'A stout man, that. I'm glad he managed to escape.'

Granville eyed him quizzically.

'I wouldn't mind betting,' he said airily, 'that you know more than you ought to about that, Windy.'

'Don't you believe it,' mumbled Storm, burying his nose in a tankard.

In point of fact he had deliberately engineered the Englishman's escape, and had even financed it. The man had lost everything that he had tried for – and no matter what his aims Storm had both admiration and respect for him; as he had for Frank Granville. He was still wondering at the cleverness with which the younger man had played his hand, although there was nothing he could blame himself for in his one-time views of Letty's brother. He realised, too, that the only reason the affair at Ledsholm had reached its murderous height was the almost fatal seizure of Number One of 'Z' Department. Craigie had been desperately close to death's door while the report from Granville – or Number Twelve of the Department – had been waiting for his attention.

But it was over. Redhead was smashed. Zoeman's organisation was broken, and all but a little of the hoard of stolen wealth had been recovered from the wreckage at the Grange. Storm felt completely at peace with the world.

He swallowed his last drop of ale, and stood up.

'Where are you off to?' demanded Roger Grimm.

Storm's beam spread.

'That's a secret, cousin of mine! I've fixed up with Horrors to give you lads a blow-out, and you can use up the rest of the barrelful. Just have a good time.'

Those members of the party who were still active spread in a pugnacious cordon round the door.

'You can go,' said Timothy Arran ferociously, 'when you've told us where you're going. Spill it!'

Storm grinned. Granville chuckled.

'If you must know,' said Storm, 'I'm going for a rest cure. Just outside Torquay. And Granny's coming with me in case I need a best man!'

First Came a Murder

John Creasey

1

Tragedy at the Carilon Club

Anthony Barr Carruthers sat in the reading-room of the Carilon Club, Pall Mall, London West, and stared morosely at the *Morning Star*, which he held in front of him.

He had been some time locating the single line of information which he wanted, for although familiar with the sporting page, he was a complete stranger to that controlled by the City editor.

His trouble was simple. On the recommendation of a man who should have known better, he had recently purchased ten thousand one-pound shares in Marritaba Tin. Within a week of the deal, his ten thousand had sunk to five, in ten days it had been shaved to two and a half, and now it was somewhere in the region of one thousand seven hundred.

Carruthers glanced again at the damning figures in the City column, then tossed the newspaper to the floor.

His back was towards the door of the Carilon Club's reading-room, and he heard it open, but did not trouble himself to look round. Even had he done so, he would have seen only the sober figure of Rickett, the Carilon Club's secretary, and would not have been conscious of any immediate danger.

Rickett was a typical club secretary, a shadowy individual who was never obvious but always present, rarely speaking, but always having the last word.

As Anthony Barr Carruthers sank back in his armchair and cursed the name of the man who had advised him to buy Marritaba, Rickett moved silently across the room. His suede shoes made no sound on the thick pile carpet, and his breathing was soft and regular. His right hand was in his trouser pocket.

A sudden breeze, coming through the wide-open windows of the reading-room, carried a blast of sultry air into Carruthers's face, and jerked him into irritable motion. He snapped his fingers viciously.

'Damn Riordon!' he muttered aloud. 'I reckon he fleeced me...."

Had he turned at that moment and seen the strange, unquestionably evil smile on Rickett's face, he might have saved himself from the undreamed-of peril. For Rickett was within a yard of him now, moving silently, furtively, towards Carruthers's chair. His right hand was half out of his pocket, and the slanting rays of the sun, coming through the open window, glinted on steel.

As he drew nearer, Rickett stretched out his hand. If Carruthers had thrown his head backwards, he would have felt the sharp prick of a needle in his scalp, and might yet have saved himself. But he kept still, unthinking, unsuspecting.

Then Rickett thrust his hand out, sharply, stabbing the needle of the hypodermic syringe into the fleshy part of Carruthers's neck, pressing his thumb firmly on the lever.

Carruthers gave a sharp cry, and swung round in his chair. In his last moment of consciousness he saw the face of Rickett, twisted in that strange smile.

'What the devil!' gasped Carruthers.

He tried, desperately, to jump to his feet, but his limbs were paralysed—then, with one convulsive shudder, he slumped back in the chair.

Rickett moved quickly over the prostrate body of his victim. He felt Carruthers's pulse, and found only the stillness of death. Without a second glance he turned away and hurried out of the room.

Love John Creasey?

Get your next classic Creasey thrillers for FREE

If you sign up today, you'll get all of these benefits:

1. The John Creasey Starter Library – a complimentary ebook, THE DEATH MISER (usual price £2.99)

2. Details of the new editions of his classic novels and the chance to get copies in advance of publication, and

3. The chance to win exclusive prizes in regular competitions.

Interested? It takes less than a minute to sign up. You can get the novels and your first exclusive newsletter by visiting www.johncreaseybooks.com

Printed in Great Britain
by Amazon